Contents

Chapters: Pages:

The Last Train from Mariupol

''If happiness is the goal – and it should be, then adventures should be a top priority.''

Richard Branson

I. An Evening at the Harbor Cafe

The raindrops were dancing on the roof of the minibus I was riding in, on my way to meet my ex-pat friends at the Hotel Europa's cozy 'Harbor Cafe'.

The hotel wasn't far from the coast, just off the Primorsky Boulevard. Its terrace provided a partial view of the Sea of Azov, and it was a popular hangout of the foreign community in Mariupol.

It was late on Thursday afternoon, and I knew some of my friends would already be there. These meetings had provided us ex-pats with a chance to unwind, have a few laughs, and exchange the latest gossip from our daily lives in Ukraine.

While many ex-pats were married, most of us single guys were dating local women. Not only because they were quite attractive, but also because they were generally very pleasant to be around.

On many occasions, during our evenings at the café, the presence of young Ukrainian professionals as well as friends made our get-togethers even livelier.

I had never come across such a closely-knit, friendly bunch of ex-pats in Kyiv, where I first arrived a year earlier, and where I was supposed to be based. And there were many more foreigners, nightclubs, bars, and cafes there.

That's why I decided to move to Mariupol in the first place, a couple of months earlier. Having visited my Austrian friend Herbert, who had already been living there, and having been invited to a couple of wild parties by him, I already knew there was a lot of fun to be had in this picturesque coastal town, full of young, optimistic, and enthusiastic people. Furthermore, it had the feel of a frontier town, with all the adventure and mayhem that comes along with it.

There is no freedom without an element of danger.

At least that's what I had already learned through experience. Even children face a greater risk of suffering an accident, each time they venture into a playground. The trouble is they usually feel freer, or even happier there, than in the relative safety of a house, or the confines of a school. Taking a risk is a fundamental part of life, whether we like it or not. Be it in business, sports, relationships, or travel. Without it, no great things can be achieved, and no great excitement can be found. And it was yet another reason I decided to leave Kyiv, and move to Mariupol.

Being a freelance journalist requires traveling, and taking some risks anyways, and that's why it didn't really matter whether I lived in Kyiv or not, as long as the publications I had been working for didn't find out. By moving to Mariupol though, I'd have to run the gauntlet of their anger, if they did.

The minibus driver kept announcing the stops in such a blurred, casual manner, that I was struggling to keep awake, on such a gloomy, rainy day. Fortunately for me, the driver seemed to have a penchant for racing, and his erratic driving helped me keep my eyes open, each time I was about to snooze. He braked intensely whenever approaching a stop, then accelerated with full power, when departing. Anyone not holding tight risked being flung around, or even landing on the floor. Finally, I recognized the stop's announcement and sprung to my feet.

Half asleep when getting out, I stepped right into a puddle, and let out a quiet curse in English, to the amusement of nearby students.

Even though I hailed from the Czech Republic, commonly referred to as Czechia, I completed my degree in journalism in Britain. Then, while working for several English language publications, I spent the past decade on the road, using English far more frequently than my native Czech, on a daily basis.

Being in Ukraine, however, I made every effort to improve my Russian, as not everyone here spoke English well, especially older people.

My knowledge of the Czech language made it easier for me. This didn't mean though, that my ex-pat friends could not speak Russian.

In fact, most of them spoke at least basic Russian, and some of them spoke fluently. Herbert, for example, spoke almost like a native. After all, the lingua franca in Mariupol was Russian, as in most other Ukrainian cities east of the Dnieper River.

True, many of my friends had moved to Ukraine years ahead of me, so it wasn't that surprising, that I had some catching up to do.

Normally, I'd be transferring to another minibus at this stop, but today was a rainy day, and because my foot was soaked in muddy water, I decided to take a cab. Not like it cost an arm and a leg in Ukraine either.

The cab driver wasn't impressed with the roll of 70 Hryvna I had placed in his hand upon arrival. He was expecting a more commensurate tip for such a muddy ride, so he just gave me a nasty look, and sped off.

As I was walking up the steps to the café, located on the first-floor terrace of the hotel, I could already hear Herbert's loud, flamboyant voice, speaking in Russian. And along with it, the subsequent laughter emanating from anyone present in his company, at that moment. It was a familiar scene, and it made me feel like going there all the more. I was a regular by this time, and so were at least four other ex-pats, their girlfriends, wives, or friends.

As soon as they saw me, I was greeted with the usual teasing, like every other member of this troop upon their arrival. "Hey Tomas, how's it hanging?" "Got wet, didn't we?" They said teasingly.

I put my wet jacket on the hanger near our table, took a seat, and removed my wet shoe. This elicited a few laughs. Everyone knew what the streets of Mariupol could turn into, during a heavy rainstorm. It was only August, with the weather still balmy, so I knew my shoe would dry in no time. "How's Anna doing"? Asked Herbert with an impish smile, knowing full well I kind of fancied her. Anna, whom I had met by chance at a shop in my neighborhood, lived in an apartment block next to mine. I once pointed her out to Herbert, while we were walking near my apartment block. It was quite a while ago, but Herbert had a very good memory for such things.

Nikolai, the burly bartender, manager, owner, bouncer, and caretaker all in one, brought me my usual double espresso with milk without asking, as always.

He only spoke limited English, so we tried to speak with him in Russian, whenever possible. He was an ex-military police detective, born and raised in Mariupol. The son of a Russian mother and a Ukrainian father. Being a Ukrainian of mixed ethnicity, he was proud of his Russian heritage but displayed strong Ukrainian national affiliation. The word was out he had taken part in the defense of Mariupol seven years ago when the separatists tried to take control of it. In this eastern part of Ukraine, culturally speaking, there was a thin line between being Russian or Ukrainian. Politically speaking, however, the difference between Russia and Ukraine was far more pronounced. And considering the recent events in this part of the world, many inhabitants of this city let their loyalties be known.

Over the weekends, Nikolai always had an extra waitress helping out at the café, as well as an extra cook helping his wife, Natalia, in the kitchen. This made for a smoother and faster service, but was not usually necessary on weekdays, apart from special occasions.

The way this cafe was run, the behavior of the staff, the relatively good quality of the coffee and food, the affordable prices along with its location gave it a very pleasant, cozy feel. A home away from home, for many ex-pats.

It took less than ten minutes to walk to the beach, and that was another reason why this café became our favorite haunt. Furthermore, those under the influence, unable to drive home, simply booked a room at the hotel for the night. It happened quite frequently, especially to Herbert. He even had a specific room for such an occasion, and the reception staff always kept it in reserve for him, as long as they could, just in case.

I settled at the large table among the others and sipped my first double espresso. It was gone in less than a minute, as usual. Nikolai already knew this, and duly brought another one in a timely fashion. I always accepted it, even on the rare occasion I didn't really want another.

Most ex-pats here were highly educated, qualified, and had good steady jobs, unlike me.

Herbert was in charge of modernizing the Mariupol Port's logistics, financed by the IMF. An impressive position for someone who barely turned thirty-six and looked younger still.

As such, he was given a large house with a nice garden, in the best part of town. He had a house cleaner and a company car for his use 24/7. Even an expense account!

Jack the Scot was an ex-SAS soldier in his mid-fifties. Bulky and muscular, with silver hair and a matching trimmed mustache, he was in charge of training the newly established Ukrainian Special Forces.

Jeremy was a young, good-looking Frenchman in his late 20s, supervising the allocation and distribution of EU grant money, earmarked for modernizing Ukraine's telecommunications systems, and metallurgical factories in

Mariupol. These guys were all specialists in their field, while I was a mere freelance journalist. Yet, none of them seemed stuck up, or arrogant. Quite the contrary.

They all seemed cheerful, open-minded, and friendly folks.

Despite Ukraine having experienced tense relations with Russia during the past decade, few of the locals I had met here seemed to harbor any anti-Russian feelings or prejudices. Not against the Russian people that is. They were wary of the Russian leadership, however, and rightly so. Later that month, some Russian forces began to assemble along the border with Luhansk and Donetsk. Most people in Mariupol, including my ex-pat friends, felt they only came there to boost the morale of ethnic Russians in the separatist regions, and not much more. No one seemed to be bothered by it.

Neither was I, despite the fact my grandparents had experienced a full-blown Soviet invasion of Czechoslovakia in 1968, about which I had heard a lot.

I barely finished my second espresso, and a round of beers was brought to our table, for all of us.

It was common for Ukrainian girls to drink beer as well, much like in Czechia, or elsewhere in Europe. They drank perhaps only a tad less than the guys, but drink they did. "Cheers and 'Na Zdarovie'", we all exclaimed cheerfully in English and in Russian respectively, to reflect our multicultural grouping.

One round followed another, the latest stories were exchanged, and before long it was dark outside. By this time I was under the influence, to say the least.

On this occasion, Jack picked up the whole tab, despite others offering to pitch in. We usually took turns, but the most well-to-do ex-pats took theirs more frequently than the rest of us.

They instinctively knew no one was out to take advantage of them, and that not everyone was earning as much as they did. We all just wanted to unwind, have some fun, and enjoy the company of the others. And that's how it was on most evenings at the Harbor Café of the Europa Hotel, in Mariupol. Just like tonight's cheerful get-together, we kept meeting here on a regular basis.

My best friend is the one who brings out the best in me.
Henry Ford

II. A Visit to the Port

Being a journalist, I was naturally curious about everything going on in Ukraine and especially in Mariupol, where I now lived. After all, I had a living to make and needed to come up with some interesting reports for the magazines I worked for, which asked me to submit more stories about Ukraine.

The clear wish of the majority of the Ukrainian people was to integrate Ukraine closer to the West. In turn, the West obliged by offers of increased cooperation, training programs, educational aids, various loans, and grants designed to improve governance, logistics, equipment, etc.

That's what most of the ex-pats I met in Ukraine were here for in the first place. And Mariupol was a frontline city so to speak, right next to the separatist regions and not that far from the Russian border itself. It was an especially important city for Ukraine due to its port facilities and the huge Azovstal Metallurgical Plant, among other things.

But it was the young people of Mariupol who especially wanted to remake this city into a modern, western-leaning metropolis. My ex-pat friends and I loved the spirit of the local people here, especially the younger ones, their friendliness, optimism, and efforts to improve their city and their country. For those reasons alone, Mariupol felt very welcoming, exciting, and enjoyable to live in. The positive attitudes of the people, despite all the hardships of the recent past, made it a rewarding place to be at. And in turn, we the ex-pats made our best efforts to help them achieve their aspirations.

Last night at the cafe I had asked Herbert if I could visit him at his office at the port to write a report for the magazine.

I can't say he was too excited about the idea at first, as he was usually too busy at the office and took his work very seriously, but he obliged for friendship's sake.

I suggested a morning time but he was only available at 3:30 pm. I took what I could get and arranged myself accordingly. I decided to sleep in that morning, with no need to get up early for such a late appointment. The sun was shining, many kids had already returned from school and were running riot in the playground of my apartment building when I finally woke up.

It was almost half-past one when I took a quick shower, then had some scrambled eggs and a cup of instant coffee for breakfast. Half an hour later I threw my laptop in my backpack, put some halfway decent clothes on, and off I went.

As I was approaching the entrance to the port facilities, where Herbert's office was located, I was stopped by a guard. "What's your name?" He asked sternly. "Tomas Slancar", I replied. "Nationality'? "Czech". "Phone number?" I had to dig it up from my phone contacts, as I never remembered my own number, having frequently changed sim cards as I traveled.

He contacted Herbert's secretary and I was let in.

Loads of workers in hard yellow hats and quite a few be-suited businessmen milled about the port facilities, while heavy machinery was moving crates and containers in the background. "What a busy port," I thought to myself.

The sounds of cargo ships blowing their horns echoed in the distance. Seagulls were flying overhead, searching for any lost piece of food dropped nearby. They were probably louder than the ships and the machinery combined as they squabbled and fought for the leftovers.

I was guided to the logistics center, 2 floors up the elevator, and as I got out, a bright orange sign read: 'The Logistics Center CEO, MA. Mr. Herbert Zittel.'

In I went, and while I was waiting, his secretary served me a cup of coffee. A few minutes later Herbert emerged from his office, dressed in a three-piece suit, looking like a million bucks. "Come on in Tomas and make yourself comfortable. Good to see you". He said loudly. He looked very professional I must say, over six feet tall, fairly slender but muscular, with light brown hair. His large, light blue eyes were as penetrating as the latest and the most powerful Siemens X-ray machine.

Still, it was clear he was very serious about his work. His phone kept ringing and stacks of papers were all over the place. Two desktop computers kept showing graphs and various figures.

"Boy, oh boy, I could never do his job. It would drive me insane," I wondered to myself.

But he was full of energy, multitasking between different issues naturally, as always.

"So Tomas, what would you like to know about my work here, about the port"? He asked eagerly.

"Just tell me how you guys improve the existing conditions here on the ground and something about the port, so I can write an article for my magazine," I said casually.

"Very well, move over here, sit down, listen, and watch this, my friend". Herbert said matter-of-factly.

He started telling me about the increasing volume of traffic, despite the Russian Navy's frequent impediments, about how they streamline the various processes of sending and receiving cargo, the new improved loading and unloading procedures, and techniques, the new machinery supplied and paid for by the IMF, etc. He showed me the various graphs and figures. The improvements to the system were obvious to see, even for those not trained in this field, and I was duly impressed. Apparently, the port's cargo ships transported mostly coal, metallurgical equipment, steel, aluminum, etc. Before the conflict in 2014, almost 50% of the port's cargo was Russian. But after, the port was cut off from many of its main shippers in the north of Donbas.

And this is why The IMF and The EU stepped in to help out.

The port started shifting its focus away from coal and metal-related cargo, and more toward foodstuffs, such as grains and oils, as well as clay and various project cargo. It also strived to improve its logistics toward better efficiency, a job Herbert was tasked to oversee.

But the 30-minute lecture seemed like an eternity to me, and my brain signaled overload.

Herbert was very sharp and he understood human nature better than most people. He noticed it and paused.

"Had enough Tomas?", and gave me his usual broad smile. Even though I was taking notes along the way, I must have missed half of it.

"Don't worry, I'll ask my secretary to type a report along the lines of what we discussed here today. You'll get it on Monday." "Good enough?" He asked enthusiastically.

"That's fantastic! Much obliged, you've been a big help," I replied happily.

Then he glanced at his fancy Rolex watch and said: "It's almost five o'clock! Fancy a quick drink on the town"?

"Sounds great", I nodded approvingly.

I knew that it was just a figure of speech and that the word 'quick' in reality meant slow, and the singular article 'a' meant multiple drinks, knowing Herbert.

I knew that this guy did his work with pride and to the best of his ability. But I also knew he partied in a similar fashion. Everything he did, he did it well, and with passion.

Whoever loved that loved not at first sight? Christopher Marlowe

III. A Night Out

I knew Herbert could be attracted to either sex, to anyone good-looking and fun. But he also distinguished between friends and objects of his desire. He knew I was heterosexual, and we were strictly friends, albeit good ones. He knew I was fairly shy when dealing with women, while he wasn't at all. That's why going out with him was the greatest fun imaginable! Especially when we were just the two of us. Herbert had no barriers, no fear, and no shyness when dealing with people in general, and this came in handy when visiting nightclubs. The rules went out the window, as soon as we hit the town at night. I was always ready and eager to join him, and he knew it.

The one weakness he had though, was his love of Tequila. The Jose Cuervo brand was his favorite, and he developed a taste for it on his business trips to South America. Subsequently, he became virtually defenseless against it. So, in order to limit his intake, he always asked me to stop him, whenever he started to get too drunk. It was easier said than done, however. But I always tried, at the very least.

His driver dropped us off at a fancy supermarket where we picked up a medium-sized bottle and a few beers to chase it down with because they didn't always have it at local nightclubs. He had to have it before we even entered any nightclub. We also picked up a couple of sandwiches to go along with it. It was only about a quarter to seven and the nightclubs didn't really get going till about 9 pm. Because we were planning to hit the Barbaris Night Club by the beach, we asked Alexander, the driver, to drop us off at the nearby Primorsky Park to chill out and finish off the tequila first.

Eventually, I also came to like it. It sort of got me in the party mood. Besides, sitting at this park was enjoyable, with nice tree-lined sidewalks and loads of colorful, nice-smelling flowers planted all around. Not to mention the many attractive women walking by, almost continuously, on such a balmy summer night, with the sea breeze gently blowing. We kept talking, joking, and laughing, knocking back the tequila shots one by one, chasing them down with beer, till the whole bottle was gone, and the sandwiches eaten. We had the last two beers in hand. "Go in?" Herbert asked impatiently. "Let's do it," I replied readily.

We paid the cover charge, walked over to the bar area, and ordered more beer. I immediately saw a number of pretty women all over the place. There always were some at this club.

One of the main reasons I loved going out with Herbert was the fact that he was one of the most positive people I had ever met, and the funniest by far.

When it came to dating, he couldn't care less, whether his partners were male or female. He didn't care if they were Black or White, Asian or Hispanic. It made no difference to him whether they were Eskimo or Indian, French or German, Ukrainian or Russian.

With such a huge pool of potential partners at his disposal, he was always likely to score. And even though he liked to keep this a secret, he almost always did.

Located by the beach, this club was frequented by locals, ex-pats, foreign students, tourists, and business people alike.

The last time we came here, about a month ago, we sat at a table, when I saw an attractive Black girl, with huge circular earrings, and a fancy purple outfit sitting at the bar, talking to her girlfriend. Herbert agreed she was attractive when I pointed her out to him.

He knew I found it difficult to approach her, no matter how much I might have wanted to meet her.

Knowing me, he asked teasingly. "Do you want to meet her?" "You bet," emboldened by the tequila, I replied eagerly. "Follow me", he said. We walked over to them, and as soon as we came, Herbert looked her straight in the eye, and with a broad smile, he said. "My friend is completely infatuated with you, and he has never had a Black girl before, so please, give him a chance"!

Stunned by Herbert's hypnotizing eyes, which resembled those of the snake from The Jungle Book, and by the bluntness of his unorthodox approach, she recovered moments later and broke into a wide smile.

She then turned her attention to me. Looked me in the eye and asked gracefully. "Is that so"? Her beautiful big brown eyes hypnotized me in *turn, as I was trying to regain my composure and uttered back haltingly. "Yes, it surely is".*

She wasn't offended by Herbert's unusual request in the least, even though one might be, under the circumstances. In fact, she seemed flattered and even entertained by it. Anyone approached by Herbert immediately felt his words were not meant to be rude or impolite. People could sense he was genuine, fun-loving, open-minded, and cordial.

"What's your name"? She asked curiously, and took charge of the situation, convinced by Herbert's mannerism that it was a genuine, friendly if a bit clumsy attempt by me to seduce her.

"Tomas", I replied. "And yours"? "Danielle", she answered softly.

It turned out she was a medical student from Brazil, along with her girlfriend.

We ended up chatting for a while that night, during which time she politely let me know she had a boyfriend, but she didn't mind being friends. We exchanged WhatsApp numbers and I rejoined Herbert at the table. I was pretty sure that if she had not had a boyfriend, my attempt might have succeeded that night.

But tonight the night was young, and the mood was right. The weather was warm, and we decided to take a stroll through the outdoor area of the club, sipping beer, and looking for potential partners. There were many people milling around the pool area, some couples were dancing to the rhythm of the music emanating from the inside, and some were kissing in the darker areas of the terrace.

Herbert always tried to get me hooked up first, knowing full well I was too shy and hesitant to make a successful approach on my own, especially if I really fancied someone. He, on the other hand, always ended up finding a date for himself. Never missed a beat!

One thing we had going for us ex-pats was the fact that Ukrainians were very positive, fun-loving people. They were especially welcoming to westerners and wanted to remake their *country along the lines of the West. They also didn't mind practicing their English or chatting with foreigners.*

Unlike Herbert, though, I was more open to finding a long-term girlfriend, possibly a wife. As much as I liked his lifestyle and manners, it just wasn't me. Nevertheless, his attitude, flamboyant style, and sharp wit made meeting girls a lot easier, and a lot more fun for me. I was grateful for his friendship, and for all the help he gave me multiple times, and in different situations. It was awesome to have a friend like him, and I considered myself lucky to have come across him by chance in Kyiv, months earlier.

As we were sitting there on the terrace, on a starry night with a beer in hand, I suddenly spotted the kind of girl I always dreamed about.

I wasn't too drunk yet, so my eyes weren't deceiving me, I thought to myself. There she was, among a group of friends, chattering and smiling periodically. Each time she moved her head, her long blond, slightly curly hair blew in the sea breeze ever so slightly, from side to side.

She was wearing a pair of old, tight, and faded blue jeans, and an equally old, tight, and faded pink T-shirt, with something written on it in Russian. I couldn't make that out but it didn't matter. She was of average height and slightly chubby. I typed exactly. I couldn't resist taking an inconspicuous walk-by, during which I noticed she had large blue eyes, like those of a cat. I was quite taken by her. So much so, that I was even afraid to tell Herbert because I felt too nervous to walk over and talk to her. Somehow, I felt I needed more time to be ready for it. At the same time, I was afraid she might leave before I talked to her, and then I might never see her again.

I realized I needed a strong drink to get a hold of myself. "Want something stronger?" I asked Herbert eagerly. "You bet you," he grinned happily, always ready to take the party to a higher level.

I walked over to the bar and asked for two double Scotch whiskeys without ice. As soon as I brought them over, Herbert knocked his back almost instantly. "I'm going to get a couple more," he said with an impish smile. We drank two more rounds, and finally, I felt as ready as I was ever going to be. What didn't escape his eagle eyes though, despite all the boozing, was the fact I kept staring in one direction the whole time. "So, which one is it this time?" He asked jokingly. "Wow, how did you know?" Surprised, I replied. "Don't tell me! Is it the one in the brown skirt or the one in the pink t-shirt"? He observed carefully, and nearly nailed it, as there were at least five girls talking in the group. I figured there was no point in postponing the inevitable, lest she left the club before I even tried. "Good guess! The one in the pink," I admitted hesitantly.

Herbert could see I was completely taken aback by this one, so he waited until three of the girls went to the toilet, then we approached the remaining two.

As always, he looked the one in pink in the eye, and said. "My friend is completely in love with you, and he'd marry you right now"!

He obviously didn't realize how right he was this time, and I wouldn't admit it under any circumstances, at least not yet.

She smiled immediately but turned slightly red. Then she looked at me and asked in an intermediate level English. "Do you guys live in Ukraine, or are you just visiting?" "We both live here in Mariupol," I responded warmly. "That's great, how do you like it?" She asked curiously. "We love it," Herbert quickly jumped in. "And that's why the next round is on us." To make things less complicated, they all ordered Baltika-7 beer, and so did we. In the meantime, I continued talking with her. "What's your name?" "Angelina. And yours?" She asked back politely. "Tomas." "Where are you from?" Angelina asked curiously. "You can guess three times if you like," I teased. She liked the idea, and went ahead guessing, "England?" "Germany?" "Denmark?" Each time I answered in the negative. My blond, curly hair and blue eyes, along with the fact I spoke excellent English confused her, and she said impatiently. "Okay, you tell me!" "Czechia," I said casually.

She looked surprised, but sort of pleased, at the same time.

"I have visited Prague and really loved it!" She said excitedly. "Maybe you take me someday?" She asked eagerly. "You bet," I answered confidently, with a smile. In the meantime Herbert, together with the waiter, brought a huge tray of Baltika beer. We all took one, had a toast, and said. "Na Zdarovie!" From that moment on, my shyness all but evaporated. As I felt I was getting too drunk, I wanted to make sure we exchanged WhatsApp numbers before she split. She readily gave me her number, an act from which I deduced she must have liked me at least a little. At that moment, I felt profound happiness. About half an hour later, they indeed suggested they had to go. But before they did, Angelina and I had agreed to meet again, and that I would call her soon.

It was easily the best night out with Herbert to date, despite them all having been great.

Love many things, for therein lies the true strength, and whosoever loves much performs much, and can accomplish much, and what is done in love is done well.

Vincent Van Gogh

IV. Meeting Angelina

"When is 'soon'?" I asked myself curiously, as I wanted to meet Angelina sooner, rather than later. Not wanting to look too eager, or even desperate, and scare her off, I was biding my time. I didn't want to wait too long, in case she changed her mind or found another partner. "What's a man to do?" I kept anxiously asking myself.

Subconsciously, I kept checking my phone for messages with increasing frequency, as if she'd be the one to send me a message first. Deep down, I knew she would not. Moreover, I wasn't even sure where to invite her, in the unlikely event she sent me a message first. I didn't have a plan, and I simply was not ready for our meeting just yet. Since I didn't want our first meeting to be too formal or too careless and didn't understand local customs well, I figured it was better to consult my buddies.

Almost instinctively, the first friend I called was Herbert. It was Saturday morning, only around 10 am, and he still wasn't answering.

I tossed and turned in bed some more, unable to sleep. So excited, happy, and anxious I felt, all at once. Finally, about an hour later, my phone began to ring, just as I was falling asleep again.

It was the man himself. "Good morning my friend, that was one hell of a night out last night, wasn't it?" He asked matter-of-factly. "The best ever!" I responded approvingly. "Can we meet later today for a chat? Perhaps at the Harbor Café"? I suggested eagerly. "You asked for it, you've got it," he replied assuredly. "See you at around 5 pm then, ciao!" I added, and we hung up. Then I returned to my 'sleep-thinking'. In it, I imagined, I'd invite her to some nice art gallery, then to a park for ice cream, or something like that. Mariupol had plenty of both, from what I had already seen. Somewhat needlessly, I was trying to come up with the perfect place to take her to, like a junior high student. As a result of my daydreaming, I only woke up fully, in the afternoon. My apartment wasn't expensive, and on the small side, in the working-class part of town. Because I didn't have a steady source of income, I was forced to economize. It was fairly cozy and warm, but the furnishings were a bit Spartan. It had a little balcony, and being on the 6th floor, it had a decent view of the city. What I wasn't happy about, though, was the bedroom. Don't get me wrong, for a single young guy, it was just fine. But now I had Angelina to think about. And there were just two narrow, separate, Soviet-style beds with a large gap between them, in my bedroom. This presented me with a potential dilemma, for obvious reasons. After I pushed them together, there was a huge gap between the matrasses in the middle. In order to solve this potentially unpleasant issue on the cheap, I had to figure out a way how to plug it, before I could even think about spending a night here with Angelina.

The sun started turning dark red, and it was time to hit the road. As usual, I took two minibuses, the second one to Primorsky Boulevard, from where I walked the rest, to the Harbor Café. Only Jack was sitting there at this point, his eyes glassy, and a half-empty bottle of Chivas Regal on the table. "Clearly under the influence, he must have been sitting there for a while", I suspected. "Afternoon Jack, how's it hanging?" I greeted him casually." Not bad, not bad, Tomas, how about yourself?" He responded drunkenly. I told him about my hangover from last night, at which point he signaled to Nikolai to bring another shot glass. He and Nikolai were like soul mates. Jack often hung out at the café, even when no other ex-pats were around. They were from different corners of the world but had similar military backgrounds. And somehow, that created a certain bond between them.

Before I could even object to the idea, it was on the table, and Jack was pouring me a large one. "The best way to get rid of a hangover," he murmured quietly". "What the heck?" I thought and knocked it back like it was a cold Cola on a hot day. "Cheers to that, feeling a lot better already," I said agreeably. Jack and I were a fairly quiet duo, when left on our own, until Herbert finally showed up, forty minutes later.

"So, are you in love, or are you in lust?" Herbert quipped laughingly. "She was quite something, wasn't she"? I replied firmly. "She surely was!" He nodded approvingly, with a naughty grin forming on his mischievous face. "Actually, I am head over heels, I'm afraid," I admitted hesitantly. "I know you are, trust me!" He laughed. "I'm not sure how to proceed with her now. I don't fully understand the local culture", I added nervously. "Don't worry, I'm sure it will work out nicely between the two of you," he assured me confidently. "I hope you are right", I added quietly. "Trust me, my friend! Have I ever failed you? I'll see to it personally if need be". He reassured me with a loud, confident, and

cheerful voice. And suddenly, my insecurity seemed to have vanished in the air.

"Even though I am not supposed to do this, I can have a word with my driver Alexander, and perhaps he can pick the two of you up, and give you a grand tour of Mariupol", he suggested gracefully. "That's really nice of you, but I can't possibly accept that". I said shyly. "Sure you can! What are friends for? Just give him a tip at the end". He replied assuredly. Upon hearing this amazing offer, I walked over to Nikolai and ordered a round of good Georgian brandy, which I knew both of the lads liked. "Here is to Angelina," I proposed a toast, which was immediately accepted by the lads.

Herbert's offer gave me the courage to call her sooner than I otherwise would have. Being picked up in a newish, gleaming Toyota Land Cruiser, would surely add some spice to our first date plans, I thought. And the stage was set.

Friday evening was agreed upon, and a couple of days later, it was time to do the inevitable, and finally call her.

Sitting in my tiny kitchen, with sweaty hands, I was about to press her number on my contacts list. It was only Tuesday, but I decided to speak to her sooner rather than later, to make sure she'd be free on Friday.

"Oh, good to hear from you again!" Angelina answered cheerfully, and immediately boosted my confidence. "Hi there, it was really nice chatting with you last Friday at Barbaris. I'd really like to talk with you some more. Would you happen to be free this Friday around six?" I asked somewhat nervously, fearing rejection. "Let me see... Actually, I am supposed to meet my friend. But hmmm, let me talk to her. Maybe I can change that. Can I call you back in an hour or so?" Angelina asked graciously. "Sure, take your time," I tried to reply calmly, but was all but calm.

I wasn't sure whether this was good news or bad, and my insecurity was getting the better of me again. Still, the mere fact she offered to change her previous arrangement for me, was an encouraging sign. "Or was that just a clever way of getting out of it?" I kept wondering.

"If she really didn't want to meet me, she could have just deleted my number, or even ban me," I reasoned to myself. I had no choice but to do the one thing I hated doing the most, wait. It was eating me up on the inside, and with each passing minute, made me even more anxious.

Finally, the phone rang, and it was her! I let it ring three times before picking it up, to cover up my anxiety. "Hi again," I answered warmly. "Hi, my friend said it's okay", she replied casually. "I'm glad to hear that", I responded, and added. "My friend Herbert asked his driver to double as our driver on Friday evening. Do you remember him"? "Of course I do! How could I forget a guy like that"? In that case, I can show you around Mariupol, if you'd like". She suggested politely.

"I'd love to! Great idea. And somewhere along the way, I'd like to treat you to dinner, at a place of your choice." I added excitedly. "Well, it's a deal. Leave the rest to me. You guys can pick me up at the entrance of The Mariupol

State University, at 129 Budivelnykiv Ave."
Angelina confirmed boldly. "You can count on it,
and see you there on Friday at six," I added.
"See you, and have a nice evening," Angelina
said sweetly. I was overjoyed. The conversation
went way beyond my expectations, and I sensed
she was at least remotely interested in me if I
played 'my cards' right. I was so excited now,
that I knew I would not be able to fall asleep
that night. But it felt good.

The driver came to pick me up first, at 5:30 pm,
as agreed. Because I didn't want to stand out
next to Angelina, I wasn't sure whether I should
wear my jeans with a t-shirt and a pair of
sneakers, or put on a jacket with a nice shirt
and proper shoes. Since I wasn't able to imagine
what Angelina might put on, I chose the middle
way and put on a smart casual shirt, blue jeans,
and casual shoes.

As soon as we arrived at the university
entrance, I recognized her pink, faded t-shirt
and tight blue jeans. She wore the exact same
things as she did at Barbaris last Friday!

It was an early indication that she would probably be neither pretentious nor snobby. My preliminary assessment of her was correct and I felt a sense of relief.

I got out of the car, waved my hand to get her attention, and as soon as she saw me, she started walking toward the car. With a broad smile she said; "Hi Tomas, it's nice to see you again". "Likewise," I responded happily. "This is Alexander, Herbert's personal driver, and he is kind enough to drive us around as needed this evening," I explained eagerly. "That's very nice of you Mr. Alexander", Angelina said calmly and shook his hand. "Any friend of Mr. Herbert is a friend of mine", Alexander remarked, with a friendly smile. He was a typical Ukrainian man. Friendly and courteous, he went beyond the boundaries of his duty when asked by Herbert, with whom he had a very good relationship. He was far more than just a driver. A tall, burly guy in his early forties, with short black cropped hair and a trimmed mustache, he was an experienced guy who helped handle sensitive situations, and covered up for Herbert, whenever necessary. Especially when it came to Herbert's wild nightlife, partying, and the various partners he met on such occasions. It had to be kept separate from his professional life, as much as possible.

Alexander was definitely the right man for the job, in every way. While he was officially a driver, he was the unofficial bodyguard, public relations officer, advisor, travel agent, and a lot more. And Herbert saw to it that he was suitably compensated, on top of his regular salary, provided by the port.

"Would you like to eat something now, or later?" Angelina asked patiently. "Up to you," I answered obligingly. "Okay, let me show you around town a little," she suggested. "I think that's a very good idea," I answered, and let her know she was in charge. She started off by instructing Alexander, or Alex as they called him, to drive us near the Cathedral of the 'Mother of God' in the city of Mariupol. It wasn't the biggest or nicest cathedral I've ever seen, but with its golden spires, it was still large

and impressive, regardless. We walked around it, while she was telling me its history. She surely knew her stuff, impressing me with her eloquence, as well as her sense of pride. Next, we drove to see the old Water Tower. I had seen it numerous times just passing by but didn't actually know much about its significance or history.

Angelina seemed to enjoy telling me about the city's history, and I was happy to listen and learn.

"This is the old 'Water Tower' of Mariupol, an important architectural monument," she said, pointing her finger at it, moving it up and down, while she was explaining stuff, like a tour guide. "It was designed by architect Victor Alexandrovich Nielsen and was completed in 1910 in Roman and Gothic architectural styles. It is 33 meters tall and the staircase has 157 steps", she added with a sense of pride, and a smile.

It's not that I was not interested in the things she had to say. I very much was, but I could not help staring at her more than at the objects she was talking about. I guess I was infatuated by her style, intelligence, and modesty, but also by her attractive looks. "Interesting style and amazing details," I said about the tower, hiding the fact I didn't know a thing about it till now, despite seeing it numerous times before.

"Glad you like it. Would you like to take a walk in the Primorsky Park?" She asked inquisitively. "Sure I would, let's do it!" I answered readily. Hearing her suggestion, though, made me feel both glad and nervous, at the same time.

Everyone who lived in Mariupol knew it was a popular venue not only for families with kids but also for couples, especially in the evenings.

Alex dutifully obliged, and then, as we were coming in to park the car near the main entrance, gave me that look. "You lucky bastard"! Without actually hearing it, all men instinctively know the meaning of such a glance. Having met Alex several times before, I knew he was just trying to indicate what really was on Angelina's mind. Being an experienced local *guy, he could read Angelina like an open book, while I was largely unaware of the clues she was passing my way.*

The park was beautifully lit at night, by alternating color themes. The predominant color was purple as we were entering, then turning red, then blue. There were lovely water fountains, rows of flowers decorated the walkways, while the trees provided shade in the daytime, and discreet hiding places for couples at night. There were also some white, Greek-looking statues, and numerous benches to rest on. For refreshments, small kiosks dotted the whole park. The smell of flowers afforded the park a very romantic atmosphere, especially after dark. Basically, the stage was set for a romantic evening together, which I was so looking forward to, yet also slightly worried about.

It became obvious even to me by now, that Angelina would never have suggested coming to this place if she had no romantic interest in me.

So what was I so afraid of then? Normally, I was not that shy with women, especially if I didn't fancy them too much, and could pull off a date even without Herbert's help, if I really tried. But with Angelina, I felt almost petrified. Actually, it was embarrassing! We were walking and talked about nature, work, and even politics. But something kept me from suggesting that we sit down, fearing the inevitable situation. Then, as we were passing another kiosk, she said she felt a bit tired, and suggested that we sit down for a while. "Would you like some lemonade?" I asked sheepishly, trying to postpone the inevitable. "Oh, I'd love that," she replied casually and gave me a gentle smile. Freshly squeezed lemonade was a common street stall drink in Ukraine. Angelina went ahead and sat down on a nearby park bench, waiting for me.

My hands were sweaty again, facing a dilemma. As much as I liked her, I found these types of situations a bit awkward. If I kissed her too soon, she might get upset. If I didn't, she might get offended. "What's a man to do?" I was wondering insecurely. We finished drinking the lemonade, talked some more, and then I said, "I once rode my motorcycle from Europe all the way to Tajikistan." "That's amazing!" Angelina responded enthusiastically. "Would you like to see some photos?" I asked. "Bring it on," she said eagerly, and as I was pulling my mobile out of my pocket, she suddenly moved much closer to me, touched my leg with hers, and put her hand on my shoulder. "Let's see them", she said excitedly.

The idea to show her the bike photos saved me from a potentially embarrassing situation, one that might have even stopped this prospective romance in its tracks.

My failure to act in an appropriate manner under the circumstances would have been tantamount to letting a soufflé go cold.

Fortunately, that type of scenario had been averted in the nick of time, and we were now looking at the snaps and giggling. Suddenly, Angelina had warmed up to me considerably, and I was finally able to relax. "Would you take me for a ride on a bike like that someday"? She asked, looking me straight in the eye.

"It would be my pleasure, but you would have to hold me tight like this". I gently took her hands and placed them around my waist.

All of a sudden, she squeezed me more strongly, put her head on my shoulder, and asked while smiling at me. "You mean like this"? "Exactly like that," I smiled back.

By this time it was obvious we liked each other, but I was still reluctant to make the first move. Angelina then gently took my hands, placed them around her waist, and said. "And this is how you must hold me when I'll drive." Her eyes locked onto mine, and she moved her face closer to mine as if to indicate she was ready. Finally, I got a hold of myself and gently touched her lips with mine. She reciprocated, and that was an indication of things to come, which would transform my life in Mariupol.

Something about Angelina meant more to me than all my prior girlfriends combined. I wasn't *exactly sure what, or why, just felt it. We then strolled back toward the car, holding hands intermittently along the way. Poor Alexander had been left waiting for eternity. Feeling guilty, we brought him a bottle of lemon juice from one of the kiosks on the way back. "I was wondering if the two of you were even coming back this evening", he joked when he saw us. It was clear we were an item now. "I just talked to Mr. Zittel that you had disappeared in the park", he quipped with a grin. "Are you two guys hungry?" asked Angelina. "You bet", we both nodded. "Could you take us to one last place this evening?" Angelina asked. "Of course, I can", he said calmly. I was beginning to suspect Herbert had slipped him a thick roll of cash, to be so patient and cooperative. I made it a point to ask Herbert about this when we met the next time. "Very well then, can you take us to 'The Cossack Farmhouse' restaurant at no.75 Georgivska Street please?" Angelina inquired. "Let's do it," Alex obliged, and he accelerated the relatively large vehicle quickly through the mostly traffic-free, late-night Mariupol streets.*

He joined us at the restaurant on Angelina's insistence. "She must have felt guilty for having him wait so long at the park," I guessed. "Or perhaps it was a Ukrainian custom," I wondered. In any case, I didn't mind one bit as the most important part of the evening went beyond my wildest expectations. In fact, I was glad he joined. "The more the merrier", I thought. The restaurant was spacious but cozy, decorated in typical Zaporozhian Cossack style, with large oil-painted pictures of famous Cossack leaders. It still had quite a few customers in it, even at half-past eleven at night. I loved the atmosphere as much as the company I was with. It felt unique, even exotic, so full of energy. I could deduce Angelina took pride in her Cossack heritage. As the waiter was approached, she asked. "Tomas, would you like to try some traditional Ukrainian food? My favorite. Interested"? How could I say no to my new, much-adored girlfriend? "Bring it on!" I looked her in the eye and nodded. She seemed pleased that I took interest in her culture and heritage. In only a few minutes, the waiter, dressed in typical red Cossack attire, brought three identical dishes. They were called Varennyky and appeared to be plain dumplings, topped with sour cream. Less than a minute after I took my first bite, she looked at me and asked, "How is it?" with a mild smile. "Gorgeous," I replied straight away. Visibly pleased, her smile widened, and her hypnotizing blue eyes radiated with joy. "I've loved this food ever since I was a kid, she elaborated". While the dish looked simple, it tasted amazingly good. Maybe because I was so hungry, or I was so infatuated with her, or simply because it really was tasty. Most likely a combination of all three. We washed it down with a round of local draft beer. "Don't worry, I can handle one", whispered Alexander, while he was looking around, to make sure no one noticed he was about to drive under the influence. It was well past midnight, we were all full, and no one wanted to order anything more. At that point, I asked for the bill. I was amazed at how inexpensive it really was. Angelina had ordered one of the least expensive items on the menu, on our first date. While there was nothing extraordinary about it, perhaps just a coincidence, to me it painted a different picture. This was a woman of integrity, pride, intelligence, and modesty. I was blown away not only by her beauty but also by her personality and mannerism.

I gently kissed her on the lips once more as she was getting out of the car near her apartment building, which looked much like mine. "Thank you", she said to Alexander, and "Call me," she whispered in my ear and disappeared into the relatively poorly lit apartment complex nearby.

I thanked Alex for his services and slipped him a 500 Hryvna tip, which he accepted graciously, once we reached my place. "Good luck with Angelina, I think you found a very nice girl", he said with a wink. "You think so?" I asked inquisitively. "Believe me, I know a gem when I see one". He winked at me once more and drove off.

"What a night and what a girl!" I thought to myself. I felt like I was a new person, and

suddenly, Mariupol had a whole new meaning to me.

Cossacks are the best light troops among all that exist. If I had them in my army, I would go through all the world with them.

Napoleon Bonaparte

V. A Trip to Zaporizhzhia

Apart from the fact I was now dating Angelina, not much else had actually changed in my life. But now, somehow, I felt as if almost everything had changed.

Back, when I sat with Angelina on that park bench at night, we talked about our jobs and career goals, but our conversation also strayed into our ethnic backgrounds, apart from other topics. I remember she told me she was half Ukrainian and half Cossack. But I didn't really understand, what being Cossack really meant. It wasn't clear to me what ethnicity they were, or what history they had. I heard the Cossacks were fearless, freedom-loving fighters and great horse riders. I also heard they had incessantly, and successfully attacked Napoleon's rearguard armies and flanks, during his invasion of Russia, but not much more than that. "What ethnicity were they?" I wondered. The Cossack-themed restaurant Angelina had taken us to that night only further stoked my interest. There was something mythical about them, I felt. And since the girl I adored so much was half Cossack, it intrigued me still more. That's when I decided to find out as much as I possibly could. "I am definitely in the right place for it, and I could then submit my findings to the magazine I work for. I'd kill two birds with one stone," I thought to myself.

An idea was born, one that I would pursue vigorously, and to the best of my abilities. For both private, and professional reasons, at the same time.

I picked up my mobile and called Jeremy up. "How are you guys doing? Long time no see. Do you happen to have any EU projects in Zaporizhzhia by any chance?" I asked curiously, knowing full well their programs covered all of Ukraine, and not only Mariupol, where he lived. "As a matter of fact we do", he responded politely. "When is the earliest time you plan on going there?" I inquired further. "Not until January. Why?" He asked cautiously.

"Well, I'm trying to write an article about the Cossacks, for a magazine I am contributing to. Furthermore, I am now dating this gorgeous girl I met at Barbaris, and it turns out she is half Cossack. So I thought of taking a trip out there with her, to visit an old Cossack fortress. I wonder whether we could tag along with you

on your next trip there. That'd be more fun anyway, I guess," I explained.

"Oh, I see, and Congratulations on the girl! Can't wait to meet her. Let me look in my plan book. I'll see what I can do", he replied warmly.

That same evening, I got a call from him. He said they had discussed this with his wife, and she liked the idea of all four of us making a short, holiday-like trip to Dnipro in the near future, with a stopover at Zaporizhzhia. Ostensibly, 'to check on the project's progress there'.

The next day I called Angelina to see if she'd be interested in meeting my friends, and taking a short trip to Dnipro via Zaporizhzhia, with a visit to the old Cossack Fortress and Museum there. She immediately liked the idea and said she would try to take that Friday and Monday off from work, for the occasion. Since I was almost always free, I only had to ask Jeremy to find a suitable time for this, hopefully over an extended weekend. And a plan was born.

In the meantime, I had invited Angelina to the good 'ole Harbor Café to meet my friends. We agreed to go there on Saturday afternoon, and I dutifully let all the boys know, including Jeremy. It was always a good idea for them to meet in person, before our planned trip to Zaporizhzhia together, to make sure the chemistry was right between them.

Angelina and I had met earlier that Saturday. I picked her up at her apartment complex, which I remembered very well, in a taxi. We ended up walking slowly through the picturesque Primorsky Park, not far from The Barbaris Club, till we reached the beach. From there, we walked along the beach, all the way to the Harbor Café. It wasn't more than a couple of kilometers, but we took our time and sat down for refreshments along the way.

We occasionally held hands, gave each other quick kisses on the cheeks, and dug up the odd shell, here and there. The Mariupol beach was no Waikiki or Phuket, to be sure. Not even close. But it still had that beach atmosphere, with the sea breeze blowing, and the ever-present, squeaking seagulls flying overhead.

By the time we reached the hotel's stairway, we both felt fairly tired. "I've never even noticed this place before, and I'm a local", remarked Angelina, with an expression of surprise on her face.

"Well, it's sort of hidden from the beach by these trees and that house, but you can still get a view of the sea from the terrace up there. My friends and I like to meet here to relax and have some fun. Besides, the staff is great, and the food is not bad either. You'll see what I mean," I explained casually.

As soon as we walked through the café's doors, Angelina pointed her index finger and exclaimed cheerfully. "That's Herbert over there!" "You've got that one right." I smiled and nodded in agreement. "No one forgets a character like that."

As we approached the table, I introduced Angelina to both Jack, Jeremy, and Nikolai. They all introduced themselves, shook her hand, gave me a quick approving glance, and asked us to join them. As soon as we sat down, Angelina turned her attention to Herbert and said in a soft, pleasing voice with a wide smile.

"Hello there, it's really nice to see you again. Thank you for sending your driver that evening. He was a great help." She then extended her hand for him to shake. "The pleasure is all mine. Tomas told me a lot about you. I am glad things have worked out between you two." Herbert replied warmly. "A round of beers for everyone please!" I called out eagerly to Nikolai. All my friends were great guys, who had helped me with one thing or another through the months. None more so than Herbert though.

After a while, Jeremy moved over to us and said to Angelia quietly. "So, you are the object of Tomas's dreams. He talks a lot about you these days. I heard you'd like to join us on a trip to Dnipro one of these days. Is that right"? "Sure I would. But I can only try to get a Friday or Monday off from work. Not sure I can get both.

I don't know whether such timing would be suitable for you." Angelina replied politely.

"My wife Sabrina doesn't work, and I can mostly arrange my own schedule. So I think we'll be able to arrange a long weekend", Jeremy assured her quickly. Angelina had fit in easily among my friends and was received well by them in equal measure, to my considerable relief. But my greatest joy came from Nikolai's comment. As I was walking to the bathroom, passing next to the bar, he quietly pulled me to the side, and whispered in my ear in Russian.

"Tomas, ona ochen choroshiya devochka." Translated to English, it meant she was a very good girl. It was a fair bet to say local Ukrainian men had a deeper understanding of local manners than foreigners. So I was particularly pleased with his observation. Then, as I was returning to the table area, I could hear Herbert talking loudly, and everyone around him, including Angelina, bursting into laughter in response. Herbert's presence gave the place that cheerful, optimistic atmosphere, which all *the ex-pats and locals alike needed, and craved. I often wondered what it would be like, without him there.*

In the end, Jeremy told me he found Angelina likable, well-mannered, and friendly. He thought she'd get along well with his wife too, without a doubt.

Due to all the new, interesting developments, I began to feel happier than ever. Everything seemed to have worked out fine for me in Mariupol.

I liked it better than Kyiv from the beginning, mostly due to its location by the sea, but also because my buddy Herbert lived there. And now, I even had a girlfriend I was crazy about. It seemed too good to be true.

As we were walking toward Angelina's apartment block, on our way back, she let me know she enjoyed herself a lot and felt I had good friends. "Would you like to come upstairs for a cup of coffee?" She asked boldly, to my big surprise. "And what about your folks? Wouldn't they mind such a late visit by a foreigner?" I replied, in amazement. "Don't worry, no one's at home." She took my hand and assured me. "Where are your parents now?" I continued questioning her worriedly. My father isn't around, and my mom and brother are in Batumi, Georgia. "My mom works there now," she elaborated."

"Well, in that case, I'd love to," I replied and looked in her eyes as if searching the depths of her soul. Because I knew well what this late invitation potentially meant for a new couple. I was overcome by excitement and deeply gratified she was no longer afraid of me. She had indicated she was ready to take our relationship to a new level, a more intimate one. No healthy man would refuse this type of invitation, and neither would I. We walked up the steps to her third-floor apartment. The staircase was almost pitch dark, with only a dim light on the ground floor. She searched her purse for the keys, opened it up, and switched on the lights. Then, she said, "here we are, and make yourself comfortable"!

She then pointed me to the living room sofa, and I was overjoyed. It made absolutely no difference to me that the apartment was very modest, the furniture most likely still from the Soviet days, because it felt warm and pleasant. I even liked the smell of it. In fact, I loved everything Angelina touched, so coming here merely enhanced my senses. "How much sugar do you like? One lump or two?" Her voice echoed from the kitchen. "Two please," I called back. A few minutes later, Angelina walked in with the two coffees, wearing just a short skirt and a red t-shirt. I could hardly take my eyes off of her. I struggled not to stare at her skirt and legs. But my eyes kept straying, and I had trouble controlling myself. Innately, she understood this, like most women naturally do. Perhaps that was the very idea. "Now that we are a couple, it is perhaps not so impolite for me to stare anymore," I reassured myself.

But my instincts were telling me she didn't mind it anymore, at this point. In fact, she may have dressed that way on purpose to get my attention. I kept sipping my coffee, trying my best to make regular small talk, and pretend that everything was as normal as usual. But nothing could be further from the truth, and she wasn't born yesterday to not know. A minute later, she suddenly took the coffee cup from my hand, put it clumsily on the living room table, sat right next to me, and started deep kissing me. Immediately, I threw the pretense of good manners out the window, put my hand around her waist, and held her body against mine firmly. We started making wild love on that sofa, without any restraint, from both sides. We both let go of any manners completely and unashamedly. It was absolute heaven.

Afterward, we were just lying there, squeezed together on that narrow sofa, neither one wanting to end that special moment in time. Eventually, we took a shower together, kissed, caressed, and hugged some more. "You can stay here with me tonight if you like," Angelina said softly, looking in my eyes". "I'd like nothing more," I whispered back gently.

I was only woken up by strange sounds coming from the kitchen, early the next morning. As if someone was saying hello, how are you, in Russian. "Kak dela? Zdravstvuj"! I was terrified, thinking her mom, or brother had returned from Batumi unexpectedly. Surely, I didn't want them to see and meet me like this, for the very first time. I started tugging on Angelina's nightgown, but she wasn't waking up. So, I whispered in her ear. "Wake up, wake up, someone is in the kitchen!" She then opened her eyes, took a brief listen, and laughed quietly. "Don't worry, it's okay. It's only Tulko." She said sleepily. "Who's Tulko?" I pressed her worriedly for an explanation." The parakeet. Don't you know?" "I didn't know you had a parakeet. You didn't tell me last night". Relieved of my anxiety, I smiled and kissed her gently. "Why was he so quiet last night then? "I pushed for a better explanation. "He's old, and he was probably asleep. We came very late last night," she murmured sleepily.

The lazy morning cuddles and hugs eventually turned into passionate lovemaking, after which

Angelina prepared a breakfast of scrambled eggs and coffee. As we were munching on it, Tulko kept flying around, occasionally landing on our plates like a Kami Kaze pilot, pecking off pieces of eggs and bread, occasionally 'shriek-talking' "Kak dealat"? (How are you?) And "Sposibo" (Thank you) in-between". Tulko, a seven-year-old male blue, and white budgie was a beloved family member. He literally joined us for breakfast. It was so funny. I was in seventh heaven. Despite the fact I wasn't really ready for a serious relationship due to my financial situation, I couldn't help the feeling I was really falling for this girl.

On Wednesday, Jeremy called whether we wanted to go to Dnipro on Friday. After making a hasty phone call to her school, Angelina and I agreed. So, on Friday morning, Jeremy and Sabrina picked us up in their blue Renault Meganne station wagon, with the European Development Fund's - 'EDF' logos on its doors. When I asked about the logos, Jeremy informed us that the EU was actually the largest aid donor in the world, to the tune of some 50 billion USD per year, right around the world, including Ukraine.

This was the first time the two girls met in person. They quickly exchanged the usual pleasantries in Russian, and off we went. Along the way, we passed numerous traditional villages, many picturesque with brown wooden houses and painted decorations around their windows. For all their traditional beauty and charm though, it was inescapable they all needed investments in infrastructure. And that's exactly why Jeremy's mission in Ukraine was justified, and much appreciated by the locals. And by the same token, I was there to help spread awareness about it, for all to see. While my mission wasn't as vital as Jeremy's, it was important and needed, nevertheless. At least that's what I liked to tell myself.

We were now approaching the city of Zaporizhzhia. It was the legendary birthplace and stronghold of the Cossacks, dating back centuries. The fact my girlfriend, possibly my future wife, derived her heritage from this place made it a trip worth taking for me. "Wake up Angelina, here we come," I whispered in her ear quietly, but anxiously. With her head rested on my shoulder in the back seat of the car, she began to slowly perk up, watching the landscape go by, with her beautiful, sleepy eyes.

We could see the car's navigation system pointing us toward the Khortytsia Island, located on the Dnieper River. We were a stone's throw away, and the silhouette of the mighty, reconstructed 16th century Cossack Fortress rose on the horizon. "I've heard all about it, but have never had the chance to actually visit this place! So nice to be here, and thank you all for making it happen for me," Angelina said gratefully. Her Cossack background was from her deceased father's side, and thus this visit had extra emotional meaning to her. A fact not lost on us all.

This Historical and Cultural Complex, the 'Zaporozhian Sich', perfectly recreated the image and atmosphere of the ancient Cossack capital.

It was a sprawling, impressive town museum, which opened in 2009. Its wooden structure harmoniously blended into the surrounding landscape and it was now one of the most famous attractions of this city. We must have walked around for hours, climbing into the watchtowers, with incredible views of the Dnieper River with the countryside on one side, and the city on the other. We took numerous photos, and read the various inscriptions. I learned a lot more facts about the Cossacks, their history, and even their ethnic makeup. They were a mix of various Turkic peoples, Tartars, Ukrainians, Russians, Greeks, as well as various other tribes which had passed by, settled, and eventually assimilated. They were a supra-national city-state, a mighty multi-ethnic cavalry, defined by their way of life, and not their nationality. In a way, they resembled today's European Union, the USA, or The Roman Empire before them. Angelina was mostly cheerful, but occasionally emotional, during our walk-around. She felt proud and happy that I took interest in her background like this, and that drew her ever closer to me. I now knew why her choice of that Cossack-themed restaurant in Mariupol wasn't just a coincidence.

Later that evening, tired by the day's events, we checked into a modest three-star hotel in town, and then had dinner in its restaurant. By now, Sabrina and Angelina were hanging out together constantly, chatting almost non-stop. After all, they had more in common than met the eye. Sabrina, too, was of mixed ethnic background. Half Ukrainian, a quarter Kazakh, and a quarter Russian. The trip seemed to have cemented a close bond between our two Ukrainian soulmates. Their conversations began to resemble ones only old friends could have and grew in intensity after a few glasses of wine and a delicious platter of Nalisniki, which we all shared that night. Our evening get-together felt more like a party and continued well into the wee hours. A lot longer than we had originally anticipated. After an amazing and eventful day, with yawns starting to appear on our faces, it was time to hit the sack.

Slightly drunk, but feeling happy, Angelina and I just hugged in bed for a little while, after which she snuggled up to me, and fell asleep in my arms. "She looked so cute," I thought to myself. In fact, I liked her so much, that I was even afraid to let her know, so as not to scare her off. But there was no longer any doubt in my mind that she liked me a lot too, possibly even loved me. I felt it.

With the events developing so positively in my life here, I was beginning to contemplate staying in Ukraine much longer than I had originally planned. Marrying Angelina, if she were interested, was no longer just a passing thought for me.

We all got up so late the next morning, that we only left for Dnipro after lunch. I no longer paid as much attention to this town as I did to Zaporizhia. I was now completely fixated on Angelina, and her happiness. Seeing her happy at the Cossack museum made me feel vindicated, and I now realized that her happiness was mine too, almost in an equal measure. Dnipro, a medium-sized town was nice, but of no particular interest to me. It didn't matter though, because I enjoyed the trip, the ride, and above all, the company. Jeremy turned out to be an even better friend than I had already considered him to be, and Sabrina wasn't the possessive wife some of my ex-pat friends thought her to be either. They just didn't know her that well, I figured.

Upon arrival in Dnipro, our hotel had already been booked, and even paid for, by the aid agency Jeremy was working for. A very nice surprise, especially for me, as I didn't enjoy the kind of steady income most of my ex-pat friends did, Jeremy included. Usually, I did make decent money from the various publications I had worked for, but it wasn't on a regular basis. So I had no choice but to economize, wherever and whenever I could. Of course, I did not do this when I was with Angelina. No way! Still, the free hotel was a welcome bonus, nevertheless.

Once we settled in at the hotel, the ladies decided to check out a local shopping mall, *looking for things they could not easily find in Mariupol. They went out arm in arm, looking like two giggling classmates. In the meantime, Jeremy and I decided to have a couple of drinks at a nearby upmarket joint. A good place to have a small chat, smoke Cuban cigars, and above all, relax.*

Even though Angelina had several good friends in Mariupol, I was glad to see her befriend Sabrina like this. It would only make my friendship with Jeremy easier.

Cuban cigars were always my favorite pastime, but I couldn't always afford them in Europe. But here, in Ukraine, they were affordable, just like almost every other item. "Angelina seems like a really nice girl for you," Jeremy observed. "And I noticed Sabrina enjoys her company too", he added. "I am very glad to see this too, and I think I love her," I proclaimed boldly. "Well, if things continue like this, she may even be the one for you then," Jeremy suggested. "You are reading my mind," I replied eagerly.

Jeremy was a devoted family man, and he didn't go to the Harbor Café with the same frequency as Herbert, Jack, or the other ex-pats, including myself. And I could easily understand why. "Who knows, maybe one day I might lead a similar lifestyle if my relationship with Angelina stayed the course", I speculated.

On Monday morning, we all went to check on the waste disposal plant, for whose modernization EU grant money was allocated by Jeremy. I took notes and tried to remember as much as possible. This was the perfect material for my articles, which I then sent to the various European publications I was a contributing writer for. It was because of those publications that I was in Ukraine in the first place. So while I was not interested in Dnipro the city so much, I was certainly interested in the factories there. I didn't dislike Dnipro either, to be clear. It was quite nice. But on its own, it just didn't interest me that much. Once our business visit in Dnipro was over, we drove straight back to Mariupol. Sabrina turned on some local music on the car's stereo system, and the miles were just passing by. Angelina fell asleep on my shoulder, just like a house cat would. Somehow, I really liked it. I occasionally stroked her hair and gave her slight kisses on the head, cheeks, and her cute, smallish nose too. Funnily, every time I gave her a kiss on the tip of her nose, she broke into a slight, sleepy smile.

The clock struck six when we arrived. The girls gave each other farewell kisses, and we all agreed to meet in town, at a time yet to be arranged.

The meeting of two personalities is like the contact of two chemical substances: if there is any reaction, both are transformed.

Carl Jung

VI. Introductions

Since returning from our trip, I couldn't stop thinking about the possibility of living together with Angelina. The apartment I was renting just wasn't adequate for a young couple, I concluded.

We'd need something a tad larger, and a bit more modern, at the very least. Angelina's apartment was a lot nicer and cozier than mine, that's why we always preferred hanging out there. But it wasn't hers either. It belonged to her family, and they were permanently returning to Mariupol at the end of the academic year, in June. These thoughts were weighing heavily on my mind. After all, most of my ex-pat friends were either living in their company-provided accommodations free of charge or in their own, fairly upmarket apartments. All of them were substantially nicer and bigger than the one I was renting.

Increasingly, because of Angelina, I felt under pressure to remedy the situation. As long as I lived alone, and didn't have a steady girlfriend, it didn't matter at all. But now that I had a nice, steady girlfriend, it began eating me up on the inside. That prompted me to contact a local real estate agent.

After consulting one, we checked out several apartments in town, to see what the going rate was. I didn't tell anyone about this just yet, it was strictly for my own information, in case our relationship became more serious. As it turned out, the prices ranged from around 30.000 USD for modest, small, Soviet-era flats, all the way to 150.000 USD for large, modern, newer ones. What I had in mind was a newer apartment, but at the lower end of the market segment. One I could possibly afford, with a little help from my parents. "In order to afford anything better, I'd have to write a best-selling novel, an unlikely prospect by a long shot," I kept thinking.

Eventually, I ran across a nice two-bedroom apartment still within my price range, built in the post-Soviet period. It had a more spacious kitchen, better insulation, and a newer elevator. Not surprisingly, it was also more expensive. But it still only cost 39.000 USD, relatively affordable by EU standards. I liked it a lot, but unfortunately, was not ready to make the purchase.

As a freelance journalist, my income wasn't all that bad. My savings of over 27.000 USD was not nearly enough. And who was going to give a mortgage to a foreign freelance journalist in Ukraine? You guessed it, NO ONE! And Angelina didn't have much savings, either. For an art teacher, who barely turned twenty-two just over a month ago, I could not expect anything else. That job could only provide her with a modest income, as was the norm in Ukraine, at this point in time. So naturally, I could not count on her with this. My best bet was to ask my folks for a loan, and then re-pay them, gradually. In fact, this was the only way. But before I'd proceed, I'd have to be sure our relationship was rock solid and geared up for the long term. Now that I had a deeper knowledge of the housing market, I'd be better prepared to make the move, should a suitable apartment be found.

After the return from our trip, I thought it was a sensible idea to give Angelina some breathing space, and only invited her to my apartment for dinner a couple of days later.

Having often heard interesting stories about her best friend Olga, and knowing how fond Angelina was of her, I invited them both. Since Angelina had not visited my apartment yet, and I hadn't met Olga, the dinner invitation seemed a suitable opportunity for both, killing two birds with one stone.

I did feel a bit conscious about the apartment though. It was fairly Spartan in terms of the furnishings, and rather small compared to hers, or those of my friends. That's why it took me so long to invite her. Our apartment buildings were only a couple of bus stops apart, and they were both of the working class categories, so it wouldn't be too much of a shock for the girls, I guessed. Once they both accepted my invitation, I sprang into action and started getting ready for the occasion.

At an upmarket shop in town, I bought good Italian pasta and tomato paste. Strangely, I always preferred Mozzarella to Parmesan and mixed it with the tomato sauce, which also included garlic, onions, and ham. I didn't think the girls would care, or even notice. After all, I was no Michelin star chef, and they weren't snobs either, so it was all good, I figured. Penne was my favorite type of pasta, and I was fairly good at preparing it. Several friends had actually given me compliments on it, through the years. I also picked up a bottle of red Italian wine to go with it, in order to create a bit of an authentic atmosphere. All was ready now, for tomorrow.

The girls had shown up on time, as agreed, and their giggles were echoing throughout the empty staircase of my old, Soviet-era apartment building. They didn't have trouble finding it either. Most of the old apartment blocks were quite clearly marked, with predictable, logical order. I opened the door just as they were getting ready to push the bell. "Hi there, nice to see you both," I welcomed them in warmly and stole a couple of quick kisses on each of Angelina's slightly chubby, cute cheeks. She smiled brightly, kissed me back, and introduced her friend. "This is the Olga I told you so much about, my best friend from school days".

"Very nice to meet you, Olga," I said eagerly, as I was shaking her hand. "Please, come on in, and sit down." I pointed them toward the kitchen table and noticed they both used the same lipstick gloss, a sure sign of their close friendship.

We started off with a bottle of Cinzano Bianco, which I still had left in my fridge from a month ago, and knew most women liked it due to its sweet taste. Sure enough, my two special guests enjoyed sipping it, while I was finishing the pasta. The sauce had already been prepared, sitting in a pot on the gas range. "Just give me twenty minutes, and dinner will be served," I announced cheerfully. "Smells very nice, and we are both hungry after work", Olga said sweetly.

Shortly afterward, Angelina turned to me, and asked; "Can I see your apartment while the pasta is being cooked"? I gave her a quick tour, but there really wasn't much to see. It wasn't lost on me that she was a bit underwhelmed by it. She remained very diplomatic, however. "It's nice", she said in a mildly unconvincing manner, knowing her. This subtle, but unmistakable hint, further impressed upon me the fact that I was absolutely right to have started thinking about getting us a better apartment, and now my suspicions had been vindicated.

"You know, I've had a look at some apartments in town, the last couple of days," I whispered in her ear. Even though he didn't say anything in response, her body language did. A gentle smile and a spark in her eye assured me, that she was pleased to hear the news. Being modest and polite as she was, she didn't make any additional comments. "Undoubtedly, she didn't want to hurt my feelings, after such a nice dinner," I thought. She didn't need to, because she already knew I noticed. That was enough for her.

"It is only natural for a woman in love to seek a nice place to live in, possibly raising a family there", this quick thought ran through my mind.

Moments later I announced victoriously; "Dinner's ready," and started serving the penne. "Help yourselves to the sauce!" I added as I was passing the saucepan around.

Then I opened the wine bottle, poured the wine into three fancy wine glasses I had prepared beforehand, and we proceeded with the dinner. "That's very good," Olga said gracefully. "Didn't know you were such a good cook", Angelina quipped. "You've got to do this more often". After dinner, we continued sitting around the kitchen table chatting. It turned out Olga was born in Mariupol after her parents had moved here from Sochi, decades ago. Naturally, she felt to be a Ukrainian but had an affinity for all things Russian, and she loved visiting her grandparents in Sochi. Apparently, Sochi was a beautiful city with balmy weather, all year round. Considering Olga was very attractive, I quietly suggested to Angelina that we should perhaps introduce her to Herbert at some point. It was a suggestion Angelina liked, she thought the world of him.

Before leaving, in a typical Ukrainian fashion, both girls helped me clean up the kitchen. It was a custom most ex-pat men grew fond of, unsurprisingly. They thanked me for the dinner again, and after Angelina opened the door, she took my hand, gave me a sweet short kiss on the mouth, and said. "Call me tomorrow!" Tomorrow was Friday, and I could not wait till I saw her again. First thing in the morning, after waking up at around ten, I sent her a big red heart emoticon, to which I received a prompt reply in the form of the words "I miss you too" with a smiley in dark shades.

We ended up agreeing to meet on Saturday morning. She wanted to show me some more places in Mariupol, which we didn't have time to see during our first 'city tour,' that evening with Herbert's driver Alexander.

On Saturday morning I was waiting for her at a bus stop near her apartment block. Angelina had decided to use regular city transport for our tour that day. She appeared, wearing a long-sleeved, beautiful white summer dress with a flower pattern around the collar, and low-heeled beige sandals. "You look like a model!" I uttered haltingly, as I saw her walking towards me.

From her attire, it was easy to conclude that today was going to be a long, casual stroll around the city. That was perfectly fine by me. I didn't mind one bit, being led around town by such a pretty girl, on such a nice day.

"Just follow me around today, if you don't mind, because I want to show you the simple things in town," Angelina said casually.

We took a tram for starters. It was actually an older model of a Czech-made Skoda tram, the kind I used to take as a kid in Czechia. As such, it *felt familiar and enjoyable for me. Pretty soon we got out and walked to the nearby City Central Park. There was a giant anchor planted in the middle of the park, and I was told it was the symbol of Mariupol City. We strolled around some more when Angelina told me matter-of-factly; "You know, the weather won't be so nice and warm much longer. It's already mid-September, we have to take advantage of it, while we still can".*

"I couldn't agree more," I replied. Next, we walked by a huge, brightly colored, and decorated anti-tank barrier, placed in the park as well. "A unique 'attraction' of Mariupol, due to the recent fighting in Donbas," Angelina explained seriously. Mariupol really was special, I thought. A seaside city like no other. A poor man's Barcelona, of sorts. All the parks in this city were very well kept, and had rows upon rows of colorful flowers, of all types, making walks enjoyable.

We continued walking until we reached the Mariupol Art Museum. With Angelina being an art teacher, it was a small wonder she wanted us to visit here. The museum was fairly large and had an impressive collection of paintings and statues. Next, we went to the Mariupol Drama Theatre, in the center of town. It was beautiful and was surrounded by a meticulously kept square. As usual, Angelina told me some interesting bits and pieces about its history. Apparently, it was built as a church of St. Mary Magdalene in 1862, in its former iteration. Then, in the 1930s, it was reconfigured to be a drama theatre. "Let's see a play here one of these days", Angelina suggested excitedly. "Good idea", I concurred.

Even though it was possible for the two of us to communicate in Czech and Ukrainian, or in Czech and Russian, if absolutely necessary, it was not possible to have a normal conversation. There certainly were quite a few words mutually intelligible, but they were too few and far between to make for a smooth conversation. Because my knowledge of Russian, let alone Ukrainian, was considerably lower than Angelina's English, we ended up communicating *in English, almost always. Only when she didn't know some English words or expressions, would she try to say them in Russian or Ukrainian, for me to decipher. But because she wanted to improve her English, she was more than happy to try speaking in English. It worked nicely for us, most of the time.*

It was getting late. The sun was setting, our legs were hurting, and we were both hungry. "I have an idea", I said. "Let's have a couple of coffees over there, rest for a few minutes, and then we decide what we do next. Agreed"? "Good idea. I could use some rest too," Angelina said as if to indicate she was ready to pass the initiative to me, at this point. It had been a long day. We saw many landmarks and must have walked for miles. It also occurred to me, that this might have been Angelina's way to make me feel like living in Mariupol for the long haul. From her ideas and suggestions, I concluded, that she had probably let her instincts lead the way. Once we finished our coffees, she asked, "Tomas, would you like to come home with me? I can prepare some dinner, and we can just relax. I don't think

I have much energy left in me today." "You are reading my mind," I replied happily.

"Let's take a taxi, I could not be bothered taking busses anymore," I added.

It was getting cooler outside at this time of day, and by the time we got out of the taxi, it was fairly chili. We had spent the entire day up and about and we're glad to be back in the warm and cozy apartment of her family. "How are you doing this evening Ms. Maksymenko?" I asked jokingly when I noticed the name tag on their door.

"Oh, you didn't know"? Angelina asked with a sign of surprise on her face. "I had not noticed it before, the staircase must have been dark before," I explained. No later than we sat down at the kitchen table, Angelina asked, "care for some hot tea with honey?" "I'd love some, it got fairly chilly out there," I answered readily. Our conversation seemed to have awakened the sleepy Tulko. He began pacing up and down the cage, at which point Angelina opened it, and let him out. He promptly landed on her shoulder, *then flew up to the top of the opened kitchen door. The tea was delicious, with the honey coming from the village her grandparents lived in, around a hundred kilometers west of Zaporzhizhia.*

"I don't remember you telling me your last name either", Angelina quipped back. "Slancar," I clarified. "Oh, Angelina Slancar then. How does that sound?" She said teasingly with a broad smile, and shiny, cat-like blue eyes. It was a remark only a girl with a fairly serious interest would entertain, that much was clear to me. Besides, that's exactly what I wanted to hear. "Fancy Tomas Maksymenko instead?" I teased her back. "How about Angelina Maksymenko-Slancar?" She asked. "Maybe we both should use the combined surnames then. How about that?" I said jokingly. While we were just fooling around, something inside prompted her to come close to me and start kissing me on the mouth. We became quite passionate, and I embraced her. Soon, she regained self-control, and said; "Let's wait a while, I had started cooking the Varenniky". "No problem, we can wait," I

replied, and began to loosen my embrace of her. She then went into her room and slipped into black, semi-transparent tights and a black long-sleeved t-shirt. With her cat-like eyes, she looked like a panther. I could hardly keep my eyes off of her though. The Varenniky she had prepared that evening was almost as delicious as those at the Cossack restaurant. Tulko couldn't resist a few bites either, and descended from the top of the door, stealing bits and pieces from both our plates. I began to suspect Angelina preferred us to meet at her place not only because it was a lot cozier and better furnished than mine, but also because she didn't want to leave Tulko alone for long periods of time. It did make sense. She had certainly grown attached to him since her teen years. With our bellies full, and our legs rested, Angelina took me by the hand and slowly led me to the master bedroom. "It's my mom's, but as long as they are away in Batumi, it's as good as ours", she smiled at me impishly, and planted a kiss on my lips. We sat down on it and started kissing passionately, almost immediately. I started taking off her t-shirt, then the black tights, and slowly laid her down on the bed. We made love for hours, or so it seemed. It was another day in paradise. Small wonder I began to feel at home in Mariupol. The next morning I woke up to Angelina quietly kissing, biting, and whispering in my ear, all at once. "Fried eggs or scrambled"? It was her way of saying 'rise and shine' you lazy bum, the sun is high. "Scrambled," I mumbled sleepily. When I finally got up, I could hear her taking a shower. I quietly sneaked in, started kissing her all over without much resistance, and we started making love, once again. "Not a bad start to a Sunday morning," I thought. Afterward, we had breakfast, with our little company, Tulko. He was already seven years old, and Budgie parakeets rarely live more than eight. I did hear, however, that on occasion, they can live up to nine. Considering how well Tulko was taken care of, with love and all, he just might stick around longer. I always enjoyed eating with Angelina at her home, and Tulko only made that livelier. Interestingly, I was beginning to feel, as if this was my new family. That morning I asked Angelina if she thought it a good idea to call my folks on WhatsApp, and introduce her. Caught by surprise at first, she did seem to be pleased by it. "Yes, I'd like to", she replied cautiously. "Don't you think it may be too early though"? She asked shyly. I knew her body language fairly well by this time, and she was not fooling me. She wanted to meet them. I also knew my dad would love to see her, as I had already mentioned her to him a couple of times. "But let's do it somewhere outside, somewhere nice", she added. We hatched a plan to go to the Mariupol Pier. It was a long, newish pontoon bridge, and it would give a very nice, holiday-like background to the introduction, we agreed. The weather was still balmy, so Angelina put on a long brown skirt and a white blouse to go along with, to appear more conservative for the occasion. She also combed and tied her long, beautiful blond hair into a ponytail. She looked stunning, like a fashion model, as far as I was concerned. Besides, it was a good idea to dress conservatively, knowing my mom's prying eyes. But my dad would like her no matter what she'd wear, there was no doubt in my mind. We had agreed to make the call at noon, Kyiv time. With Prague being only an hour behind, this time would suit my folks as well. I was as excited about it as Angelina. If they liked her, I thought, they'd be more willing to lend me the 15.000 USD, which I'd surely need for buying an apartment. This, however, I didn't tell Angelina. I didn't want to make her feel nervous needlessly. We took a cab, almost all the way to the beach then walked the rest to the pier. It was a beautiful day, with a very slight breeze coming in from the sea and clear skies. For a few minutes before the call, we just enjoyed the scenery. A long stretch of the sandy beach, along with much of the city skyline could be easily seen from the pier, so, we stood with our backs toward the beach, to make the video call. "Hi mom, hi dad, good to see you again! How are you doing?" I said in Czech, as my folks only spoke limited English. "This is Angelina, my beloved girlfriend," I said in both Czech and English, respectively. Angelina responded by saying, "hello, it is very nice to meet you, my name is Angelina". "Both the city and the beach look wonderful", my father said in halting English, then in Czech, and I translated it to Angelina. They exchanged a few niceties, and that was enough. The conversation may have been short, my impression was they liked her, despite the fact she was slightly nervous when talking. Angelina thought they were nice people too, to my big relief. It was a very brief interaction, but it was important that they had seen, and talked to each other, however briefly. "Do you think they liked me?" Angelina enquired in an insecure tone. "I'm sure they did", I assured her with a smile. We then agreed to talk to her mom the next day, at the same time. Since we didn't need to impress her mom with Mariupol, it could be done from anywhere, except, of course, their apartment, or mine. It had to be a neutral, innocent venue. We agreed to do it from the Primorsky Park, due to its beautiful ambiance, colorful flowers, as well as its proximity to the Harbor café, where we had agreed to meet Herbert and Olga that same day. While we'd like to hook those two up, deep down we knew it would probably not work, knowing Herbert's flamboyance, and a wide variety of tastes. We just wanted to have some fun, and for that, the company of the two would be interesting. We had not seen Herbert for a while and were both eager to meet up with him. About half an hour after the call with my folks, I received a WhatsApp message from dad, with a thumb up and a message: "Congratulations, what a lovely girl! Give our regards to her, and tell her to come and visit us together with you sometimes." I immediately showed and translated the message to Angelina. She could not be happier and added; "Tell them, I'd love to visit together with you, as soon as possible". It was a major victory for us, to have my parents on board. We knew we might need their support at some point, as most young couples do. Furthermore, we now both felt it made the prospect of our marriage that much more realistic, even though neither one admitted this openly. After having some ice cream and coffee downtown, Angelina wanted *to look for some art materials for her school, and I had to catch up on my long-neglected editing and writing. We decided to split up for the day, and meet up at 10 am the next morning at the Primorsky Park entrance. We parted ways with a nice quick kiss on the lips and a hug, knowing full well we had succeeded in reaching a major milestone today.*

First thing in the morning, I put on a nice blue jacket, a light blue business shirt, black pants, and dark brown business shoes, to try to make a good impression on Angelina's mother. In contrast, Angelina showed up in the same tight, faded blue jeans, and the pink t-shirt I saw her in the night we met at Barbaris. I still could not make out the words of the faded, white Cyrillic letters, and for curiosity's sake, this time I asked her about it. "Why? It means 'Life is a Beach' in Russian", she replied, with a curious look on her face. "Because these are the same clothes you wore at Barbaris Club that night I first saw you," I explained. "So you remembered"? Angelina was overjoyed, came closer to me, and gave me a sweet, long kiss. We didn't have a habit of saying 'I love you to each other. There was no need for it. Every normal person can feel whether they are loved, even without being told. And by this time we both felt it.

It was time to make that fateful call. I felt nervous, and Angelina could see it. "Thank you for dressing up for my mom, I appreciate it," she whispered in my ear. "Do not worry, I am sure it will be fine," she reassured me. "Hi, mom, good to see you again! How are you guys doing? Here is someone I'd like you to meet," she said in Russian. "His name is Tomas Slancar, and he is a journalist from Czechia. I was introduced to him by a colleague." Angelina told a white lie. "Oh really, that's good. He looks like a nice guy. Hello Tomas," her mom said to me, and waved her hand, together with Sasha, Angelina's nine-year-old brother. I reciprocated by saying hello and waving my hand to both of them, in turn. Angelina then spoke for a few more minutes, before hanging up. It was obvious to me though, that she had not told them a word about me up to this point. I suppose it is a bit different for a young woman, separated from *her family, and living alone. She didn't want them to worry needlessly, I assumed. It made perfect sense, so I didn't dwell on it. "It is okay, she liked you," Angelina reassured me and winked. Phew, the 'trial by fire' episode was behind us, and I felt relieved. Not even a minute had passed since the call, and Angelina grabbed my hands, looked me deep in the eye, and gave me a firm, deep kiss. This was it. The road forward for our relationship had been cleared in her mind, as it was in mine. Officially, we were an item now, and our parents had put a seal of approval on it. As important as it was to me, it seemed even more important to Angelina.*

We then continued walking slowly through the park, embracing each other, as married couples do. We both felt overjoyed by the way things had been developing around us. We felt happy and shared this wonderful feeling. I often thought Angelina went out of her way to please me, and I duly tried to reciprocate this. By now, I had decided to find a suitable apartment of my own. We both knew we were on borrowed time at her mom's place, and my rental apartment was neither mine nor suitable for our future.

"I have decided to buy my own apartment in Mariupol," I suddenly told her. "And of course, you'll be more than welcome to live there with me, should you so decide. And I hope you will." Angelina looked at me with a peaceful, pleasant expression on her face, without saying anything. She squeezed my hand more firmly, while we continued walking through the park. As if that was her answer in the affirmative, and it didn't need to be spelled out. And that's how I took it, knowing her. Having passed my WhatsApp 'family exam' with flying colors, I suggested that we take a walk along the beach, on our way to the café. We walked lazily and slowly, digging up random shells and sea urchins along the way. Under these positive circumstances, by the sea, we felt relaxed and liberated. We could now live our lives more on our own terms, and it had a magical effect on our states of mind.

Attraction is beyond our will or ideas sometimes.
Juliette Binoche.

VII. A Surprise

Having arrived at the café too early, it was still deserted. The large comfortable chairs on the patio looked tempting, so we sat down, and put our legs up on the railing in front of them. It felt so comfortable, we felt like we were lying on beach loungers. In this unusual position, Nikolai wasn't sure whether I wanted my usual double espresso or a Pina Colada, so he sent out a waitress to find out. And he was right. We ordered two pineapple juices and kept sitting there like that until Herbert showed up. To our big surprise, today he wasn't alone. He brought Andrey with him. A young, tall, good-looking Ukrainian guy with short, light brown hair, and a build like that of a sportsman. Tactfully, we didn't ask anything about his relation to Herbert, and likewise, Herbert only introduced him as his friend. Both Angelina and I suspected they might be lovers. Of course, it wouldn't make one bit of difference to us, except that in this case, we were hoping to hook Olga and Herbert up. This unexpected situation made our meeting more mysterious, and more complicated, in equal measure. But no matter what the situation, Herbert always had some trick up his sleeve. And that's why we all loved hanging out with him. If there ever had been a Greek God of Partying, no one would come closer than him. "It's nice to meet you again Herbert, and you too Andrey", Angelina said politely. "How are you two guys doing"? Replied Herbert with a wide, naughty smile, and a hypnotizing stare. Angelina liked Herbert dearly, as much as I did. She understood his character well and felt grateful to him for having hooked the two of us up. In order not to put any pressure on him, we didn't even tell him we had invited Olga to meet him today. We wanted it to look like a chance meeting, with no strings attached.

From my previous experience with Herbert, I already knew that whenever he had a good-looking guy or girl with him, like today, there was a fair chance it could be his boyfriend or girlfriend. And because it usually wasn't a long-term affair, I never asked him about it in front of other people. It was an open taboo. To compound matters further, there was the fact that Herbert had also been known to have male friends, strictly friends, because I was one of them. So, Angelina and I decided to play it by ear, and let the situation develop any which way it wanted to.

"Nikolai, four tequilas and four coke chasers please," shouted Herbert. He didn't care whether someone might not like it. And because he always created such a fun atmosphere, no

one wanted to spoil it. Everyone just went along with it. "Incredible", I always thought to myself. No one ever complained about him, not even afterward. A couple of minutes later Olga showed up. Dressed in a similar, casual style to Angelina, she didn't really know Herbert. She had heard a lot about him though. She happened to be one of Angelina's friends at Barbaris that night and had only caught a glimpse of him, on her way to the bathroom with the other girls. That's why we had to properly introduce her to him. But now that Andrey was here, we had to introduce them all to each other. Since we could not tell whether Andrey was just Herbert's friend or a lover, we simply introduced him as a friend. What we did notice in no time, however, was that he kept eyeing Olga up and down, ever so inconspicuously. And it didn't escape our attention either, that Olga didn't mind it in the least, and kept eyeing Andrey up as well. What an unexpected situation! Angelina and I giggled to ourselves when we stepped aside to presumably answer some real estate agent's *call. We had no idea Herbert would bring someone with him that afternoon, let alone that Olga might fancy him.*

But the mood was right, Olga even drank tequila, like the rest of us, which was not so usual for her, according to Angelina. She wasn't much of a drinker, and back at my apartment she had barely touched the wine I served. Andrey, ever conscious of his zero-fat-body, was chasing the tequila down with Coke like there was no tomorrow. Their mutual attraction seemed quite subtle and innocent, but it was inescapable to the observant eye. Fortunately, Herbert, unlike most other people, could care less about this development, even in case he did have something going with Andrey. He enjoyed this crazy situation along with Angelina and me, because that's what his private life was all about – F.U.N. Furthermore, he had no difficulty attracting partners, male or female. Eventually, overcome by curiosity, I pulled Herbert to the side, and quietly told him: "Those two are clearly attracted to each other, did you notice?" "You bet your mama I did", he said cheerfully.

"And we are going to help them get it on," he laughed out. "But what about you and Andrey? Did you guys have anything going together"? I continued inquiring. At this point, he smiled broadly, looked me straight in the eye, and said in an impish tone, "I only wish! He is my friend, but also a colleague. I never mess with my coworkers, no matter how hot they might be, regardless of whether they are interested or not. Much better that way, don't you think?" "Makes sense, I couldn't agree more," I nodded. Herbert had always been genuinely happy for others, and this time was no different. In the meantime, the two lovebirds literally gravitated toward each other, and pretty soon, our observations had been confirmed. A few minutes later, Olga and Angelina went to the bathroom together, most likely to have a typical girls' talk. When they emerged, Angelina pulled me to the side and told me Olga was head over heels with Andrey. Everyone could see it anyways, but now it had been confirmed. After talking with Andrey at the bar for a few

minutes, Herbert also confirmed that Andrey was interested in Olga.

It truly seemed that Herbert's presence had the effect of an aphrodisiac on all those around him. Later that afternoon, as the sun was setting and it was becoming colder on the terrace, Andrey had offered Olga his jacket, which she readily accepted, and placed around her shoulders. Angelina even noticed, that Olga inconspicuously rubbed her nose against the jacket's sleeve to sample his smell. A sure sign she had fallen for him, Angelina whispered to me quietly. Shortly afterward, we all decided to move inside.

Interestingly, but not surprisingly, as we were approaching the table, Olga followed right behind Andrey, and found herself sitting right next to him. All of this didn't escape our attention, and discreet winks and smiles were exchanged by the rest of us when the two lovebirds were not looking.

No sooner than we all settled down around our favorite table, Jack walked in. He looked quite haggard, unlike other days. "We had a tough training today. Somebody give me a double Scotch on the rocks with a soda please", he said loudly in his usual baritone, but with a smile on his face. He gave us all a passing glance, nodded his head, and then turned his attention to Nikolai again. "Where's my bloody whiskey Nick? I need one real bad," he exclaimed. "Give me a minute Jack, I'll be right out" Nikolai shouted back from the kitchen, located behind the bar. Before Nikolai even managed to emerge from behind the bar, Herbert had already pulled Jack over to the table and had given him a shot of tequila, instead. "Here, have this. It will do the trick before Nick brings your stuff, I promise you", said Herbert jokingly. "Jack knocked it back like it was the last cup of water in the Namibia Desert, and said," Brrr, I hate this stuff, but right now, anything will do," and asked for another shot. In the meantime, Angelina and I were glad to see that Olga was so keen on Andrey, even though we were caught completely by surprise by it. At around 178 cm tall, with thick, slightly curled, long

brunette hair, and piercing green eyes, Olga
was a tough make for most guys. Many were
chasing her, but she didn't seem to be attracted
to any. So much so, that she even complained to
Angelina she was not able to find any guy she
could fall in love with. "They all just want one
thing", she used to complain. And now, all of a
sudden, without so much as Andrey having to
lift a finger, she was melting. It was Olga who
fell for Andrey first, and not the other way
round. He had merely noticed it, and
considering how attractive and friendly Olga
was, went gladly along with it. Not that he
didn't like her. He did but wasn't quite as eager
as she was, at least at first. Perhaps that's what
turned Olga on, after all. Such are the ways of
the world, Angelina and I concurred. Since it
was a Monday evening, and as nice as it was,
by 10 pm, most of us had to go back home to be
ready for work the next day. While Olga was
head over heels with Andrey, it was awkward
for her to consider sleeping with him on the first
day they met. No matter how much she might
like the idea, she might send out the wrong

signal about her dignity and reputation. Emboldened by the tequila, however, she was leaning on Andrey, and could not hide the fact she felt in seventh heaven. She certainly didn't feel like breaking up this comfortable position, and rushing home, just yet. But it was getting late, and we all wanted to go by now. Herbert, Jack, I, and even Andrey chipped in to pay the bill. Herbert and Jack picked up the biggest part of the tab, with me and Andrey contributing mostly symbolic amounts. We all knew who the biggest earners were, and those guys usually did not mind picking up the biggest share. They often even refused to let us ordinary folk chip in at all. Only sometimes, when small amounts were due, would they let others pick up the tab. One doesn't find friends like these easily, I always thought. After all, it was due to dating Angelina, and having friends like these, that I decided to make Mariupol my home.

Herbert, Jack, Angelina, and I started getting up and putting our jackets on. We were getting ready to call cabs. But not everyone seemed so ready to go home, just yet. Olga and Andrey just continued sitting there, as if they had been stuck there by some kind of crazy glue. Angelina signaled to Olga to get up and come with us. But Olga seemed reluctant. "This is the highly unusual behavior of her. Unheard of, in fact. She had never done anything like this before," Angelina whispered in my ear. "I am embarrassed and worried about her, in equal measure," she added. "We can't just let her stay there. We know nothing about this guy, you know." Angelina had a point, but I had no idea what to do in this situation. Clearly, Olga liked him, and he did seem to be a nice guy. Out of concern, we turned to Herbert for help. "Why are you so worried? Can't you see they like each other? He is a nice guy! He works with me. Would I introduce you to someone bad? Don't you trust me or what? Have I ever failed you guys"? Herbert said in a slightly drunken tone. He did manage to allay Angelina's fears though. Both in regard to Andrey's integrity, and his being a heterosexual. After all, she held Herbert in high esteem and trusted him. At that point, Herbert, in his usual, extravagant, straightforward, and friendly fashion, asked out loud: "Listen up Andrey, Olga! If you guys want, I can offer you a room, right here at the hotel, free of charge. I sometimes stay in it when I get too drunk to go home. You'll have a view of the sea, real romantic. Are you both interested?" Andrey readily nodded, as expected of a man his age. At that moment, Angelina gave Olga a stern look, but to no avail. Olga could hardly hide her enthusiasm and tried her best to look hesitant. But she couldn't resist her feelings, and quietly uttered the word 'yes'. She didn't even dare to look Angelina in the eye. It was almost comical. She behaved like a guilty puppy, confronted by its master.

"But only under one condition", Herbert continued.

"I do not want to hear there was any trouble. You know what I mean Andrey"? Herbert added.

He looked at him with a stern face, as if to let him know there will be big trouble if he does something bad, something against Olga's will.

Herbert did this for all to see. But deep down, he knew it was just for the show and wholly unnecessary. Everyone with half a brain could see, that Olga was infatuated with Andrey, and was just as eager to spend the night together as he was. Still, Herbert set the rules, just in case. On the one hand, Angelina was happy for Olga, but on the other, she was quite concerned for her. She was her best friend, after all.

Then she came up with an interesting idea. "How about if we got a room next to theirs, or nearby? That way we could be ready to help her if there was any trouble. I know it is unlikely, but our presence nearby would also deter Andrey from potentially doing something bad." I thought about it for a minute and realized it was actually a great idea. At least we could also spend a romantic night by the sea, and kill two birds with one stone. "Great idea," I replied enthusiastically. Angelina gave me that big, calm smile, the kind she always did when she was happy. I asked at the reception, and they gave us a room located just two rooms further down the hallway. I readily booked it. It wasn't that expensive anyway, only around 29 Euro. "I got it," I told Angelina upon returning. She immediately walked over to Olga and Andrey and told them the news. Olga broke into a big, happy smile. She knew it was not necessary, but appreciated Angelina's friendship and concern. The guys, including Nikolai, were glad we found a suitable solution to this unusual situation. "Enjoy the night guys", Herbert quipped with a naughty smile, before he went home. Nikolai was closing the café as the four of us walked up the stairs, right past him. Olga's eyes were sparkling like the Azov Sea on a moon-lit night, as she gave us a quick glance on our way up. The funniest thing was that due to Herbert's cheerful character, both Angelina and I, and Olga with Andrey was now couples. Once we reached the fourth floor, upon which we were all staying, Andrey invited us to join them in their room, for a small chat. This was Herbert's unofficial room and was better equipped than the others. It had a minibar, the best views, and the largest bed. Andrey seemed like a jolly good fellow, and I was not worried about Olga in the least, frankly speaking. After chatting on the balcony over some sodas for a while, we decided to go to our room, and leave those two love birds to their exciting fates. We only agreed to meet them at six in the morning in the lobby, to share a taxi back.

Despite being a bit drunk, Angelina and I opened the balcony door, and against the backdrop of the calm, moon-lit sea, gradually started making love. We were in the right place at the right time. It felt fantastic, and I was wondering why I didn't get this idea sooner. Later on, we ended up randomly embracing and kissing throughout the night. Only the call from the reception woke us up. Spending such a cheerful, relaxing evening, followed by an exciting, romantic night just didn't get much better, judging by my past experiences. We proceeded downstairs, where we waited for the new lovebirds on the reception sofa. Shortly afterward they emerged from the main staircase, arm in arm, smiling radiantly. Obviously, the night went well for both of them, and our worries were no more. Olga had finally found her match.

Privacy is not something that I'm merely entitled to, it's an absolute prerequisite.

Marlon Brando

VIII. Getting My Own Place.

One nice experience after another, I was becoming convinced this was the right time, and the right place, to get my own apartment, and settle down with Angelina. I was in love, had good friends here, and Mariupol was a lovely seaside city. "That's it," I thought to myself. "I'm going to buy myself an apartment". I told Herbert, Jeremy, and even Nikolai, to keep an eye out for one, if they knew of something slightly newer, and not too expensive. I also called my dad to ask, if he could lend me some 15.000 USD for this purpose. He was a bit skeptical at first. "I know, she seems very nice, but are you sure she is the right woman for you? And what about the separatist region next door? What if that flares up again"? My mom joined in, and then kept asking me seriously. "I had never been so in love with any woman before. Angelina is the best girlfriend I've ever had," I kept reassuring them. "Besides, there had not been any fighting here since 2015, and the matter had been largely resolved between the parties." I concluded. "Ok, ok. Give us a couple of days to think this over", my folks said hesitantly. I was hoping something could be found around the Primorskyy District, close to the park, Barbaris, and the beach. I knew it was too much to hope for, but I kept an eye out for it anyways. The vast majority of apartments here were built in the Soviet–era, but a good 20 % were built after, and new ones were continuously being built. Many old ones had been renovated too, and one of those would also be fine, especially if nearer the beach. Since

I also had a lot of editing to do, I took my laptop to the Harbor Café each morning, trying to get it all done, while Angelina was teaching, and my friends were busy at work. My submissions to the various magazines were overdue, and everything needed to be submitted as soon as possible, in order to get paid. I needed to stash as much money as I possibly could, at this point. Fortunately, working at the café was relaxing in the mornings, with few people around. Each morning, I'd order scrambled eggs for breakfast, which Natalia had a very good way of making, with mushrooms and ham added. The bread was also always fresh, brought in at around 9 am every day. For some reason, I wasn't good at writing at home. I could not concentrate and get easily distracted by all the mundane tasks. Cooking my own breakfast, and then cleaning up the mess would severely disrupt my concentration, for example. Simply put, I needed to be at a café someplace in town, with fresh coffee, and eggs for breakfast. The Harbor Café had all of that, the beachside atmosphere, and the staff I knew well. If I managed to submit all four articles by the end of the month, I'd have almost five thousand bucks earned and coming my way. A decent amount toward the apartment. Then, while I was editing one morning, my phone rang. It was a real estate agent. She wanted to show me an older, but somewhat refurbished apartment in the Primorsky District, which got me on my feet at once. I took a cab to meet her there. It was located between Kronshtadska Street and Dnippropetrovsky Lane. The absolute perfect location, right in front of the Primorsky Park, the Mariupol Beach, and a walking distance to the Barbaris Club. It wasn't that far from the Harbor Café either, and if one wasn't pressed for time, one could easily walk there too. Having passed through that area numerous times before, I knew those were older, Soviet-era-style apartment blocks. Notwithstanding that I had not even seen the apartment in question yet, I was quite keen on it, for its superb location alone. However, I was also determined not to let my enthusiasm show, in order to be able to bargain for a possible discount. The agent and I went up by elevator, got out on the 5th floor, and entered the apartment. An old, widowed lady was selling it, to move into her daughter's house near Kyiv, I was told. The apartment was fairly large, with three bedrooms, and a balcony facing the Azov Sea. Never mind it was slightly dilapidated here and there and would need a partial overhaul on the inside. What mattered most was that it was the second block from the park. And from this location, we would have a view of the park, and the sea behind it. What more could I ask for? There were no newly built apartments in this particular location anyways, and it was prime real estate. A newly built, modern apartment right here would cost a fortune, no doubt. The asking price was 45.000 USD. It was more than I could afford, but a skillful negotiation could settle it. I went ahead and told the old lady, in my limited Russian, that I would have to completely renovate the bathroom, and the kitchen, and partially renovate the whole apartment, making it prohibitively expensive. She was adamant on the price, however, so we agreed to stay in touch and possibly negotiate further.

The agent promised to keep me posted on all the latest developments before I returned to the café. There, I forced myself to finish 2 whole articles before Angelina returned from work. A task I actually managed to get accomplished, so motivated was I by the apartment prospect.

At first, I wanted to keep the apartment hunt to myself. However, there was no denying the fact that if it wasn't for Angelina, I would not even bother looking for one, in the first place. After some thought, I decided to inform Angelina about everything. I sent her a message, along with the pictures I took of the apartment and asked if I could pick her up from school, so we could go and look at the apartment's location, at least from the outside. She immediately agreed and asked me to pick her up at half-past four. When she emerged from the school, she was all smiles. Once at the apartment complex, we walked around some, then I pointed out the apartment in question.

"Wow, I think it is a fantastic location, and from the photos, it looks spacious on the inside too", she said excitedly, with a smile breaking on her face. "Three bedrooms on the fifth floor?" She double-checked. "That's right," I confirmed eagerly. "It is going to be your apartment, so I don't want to meddle in it. But I think you could do the renovation gradually if the price was too high for starters. I would definitely help you out with that. You can be sure the price will only keep going up in this location, and one day you could sell it at a handsome profit. Besides, I'd love to keep visiting you here", she added excitedly.

Hearing this only prompted me to double down on my efforts to get it.

Clearly, Angelina was as thrilled about it as I was. My plans seemed to have flawlessly aligned with hers. As we were slowly walking away from the area, she suddenly put her arm around my waist and gave me that approving look. "If I buy it, I'll give you a set of keys, and you can use it as your own, rest assured," I told her boldly.

Angelina probably understood that if our relationship became permanent, or at least long-term, she'd become a part-owner. As for me, I certainly realized, that she was not in this relationship for that purpose.

That same evening I called my folks, sent them the apartment photos, and explained its location. Afterward, I tried to find out about a possible loan. "Tomas, it does look nice, and we especially like the location. It looks like you are there on a permanent holiday", they joked. "Perhaps we can visit you there, someday. Let us discuss it some more tonight and we will let you know tomorrow. Is that okay"? Mom asked cautiously.

The next morning, I arrived at the café, as usual. I barely settled into my position and started finishing the third article, when the agent's phone rang again. Apparently, the old lady had changed her mind. Perhaps because she did not have any other prospective buyers yet, she had *decided to lower the price to 41000 USD, if it was paid in USD cash, in full. Upon hearing this latest offer, I told the agent I was just waiting for a call from my folks, and as soon as I got their agreement, I'd buy it. Possibly even the next day. But it might have to be a bank transfer, perhaps even in Hryvna because it might not be possible to get that much USD in cash. The agent said she'd discuss it with the old lady, and call me back. Twenty minutes later, she called and said if paid in USD cash, she'd settle for 40.000. If paid in a Hryvna transfer, it would have to be the equivalent of 41000 USD on that day's exchange rate. It was a good offer, which I didn't want to let pass me by. As I kept waiting for my folks' call, I kept working on the third article, knowing I'd need every penny as soon as possible, in case I bought it.*

Funnily, I didn't remember a time when I had worked as quickly, as I had today. "People are capable of amazing things, if properly motivated". I thought to myself.

Angelina was my ultimate motivation, and I knew it full well. And it kept me wondering, how one ordinary girl I met at a nightclub by chance, could transform my life, so profoundly. Everything I was now doing was a consequence of it, for better or worse. It did occur to me, that the whole idea about the apartment might be premature, possibly even wrong. But considering Angelina and I got along so well, I might regret not buying it in a few years' time when I would not even be able to afford it anymore.

"What the heck, stop the worrying Tomas," I said to myself enthusiastically.

'Only a fool hesitates', (or 'Hlupak Vaha' in Czech) was the title of an old Czech pop song, and as its lyrics indicate, most people regret not having taken a chance, when it presented itself. "That's it, I am buying it, provided my folks lend me a helping hand." I had finally decided.

The call from my folks finally came late that evening, when I was getting ready to hit the sack. They had agreed to loan me 15.000 USD, and I instructed them to send it to the agent's account. They did so promptly because the agent had called me the first thing in the morning, that she had received it. I added the rest, and we signed the sale contract by noon. Unfortunately, I ended up having to pay the full USD 41.000, due to the payment being made in Hryvna. Most importantly, the apartment was now finally mine. Overjoyed, I immediately called Angelina, who managed to sneak out of school earlier, and came to meet me in the new apartment!

The doorbell rang, and Angelina jumped up in my arms. She kissed me on the cheeks, on the nose as well as on the mouth, happily. For all intents and purposes, it was now our new apartment rather than just mine, and she knew it. At least, she could now be certain I was really serious about her. That was a big part of her joy, almost certainly. "I am so happy for you Tomas, so happy for us," she said excitedly." "Me too, me too," I responded happily, pulling her closer to me, and embracing her more tightly. We stood there for a minute, holding each other, letting the fact we were now in our own new flat, sink in gradually.

There was a lot of work to be done, and a lot of things to be bought. By the time I arrived with the agent in the morning, the old lady managed to sell, or remove her old washing machine, the fridge, and a number of other household appliances. It was just as well, we had not agreed on keeping them anyway, and wanted to buy new ones. Despite having almost no furniture, or appliances in our new apartment, we just loved being there. Regardless of the fact there still wasn't anything to sit on, we decided to order a takeaway pizza, and eat it on the living room floor. Funnily, it never tasted as good, as it did now, in our new place. We just sat there on the floor, eating the pizza from the delivery cardboard box, taking turns drinking the delivered coke from the bottle. We were as happy as little kids, who unexpectedly got a new box of candy. We took numerous snaps, including selfies eating the pizza on the floor, and dutifully sent them all out to families and friends. It was that special moment of our lives, and we wanted to always remember it.

"Congratulations! Awesome! You guys don't have any furniture"? Sabrina was the first friend to respond. "Jeremy and I were just thinking about buying some new stuff for our pad. Perhaps we can give you a few items we don't need any more if you like," she added. "We'll take anything, thanks"! Angelina messaged back. Pretty soon, more messages came with similar suggestions. This was good news to us, as we didn't have much loose, disposable cash left. "I'm going to buy new beddings, and some kitchenware", Angelina suggested right away. "And I will have a new set of keys made for you, still today," I responded in kind. Next came a call from Herbert, letting me know he had an extra kitchen table he wasn't using, and that Alexander would drop it off on Saturday, along with some other stuff he didn't use or need. In turn, Olga and Andrey promised to help out with cleaning and renovating. Somehow, Mariupol now felt more like a real home, rather than the adventurous, wild frontier town I *considered it to be earlier. I loved this new, homey feeling. There was now this newfound enthusiasm in the air, which I had not felt elsewhere before, and I loved it. Angelina and I agreed to meet here on Saturday morning for the clean-up, repairs, and whatever else we could do by ourselves. Andrey and Olga were also due to come and help out.*

That evening, after Angelina went home, I had a new set of keys made for her at a nearby locksmith's. On the way back to my rented apartment, I was checking out every furniture and household appliance shop along the way. Later that night, I couldn't go to bed without thanking my parents for their financial assistance. Then, later, I could not fall asleep either. Rather selfishly, I kept exchanging various silly emoticons with Angelina, who needed to get up early the next morning for work. Fortunately, she didn't seem to mind and kept sending me even more messages. Such was the excitement we both felt that night. After getting up late the next morning, I hit the Harbor Café again, to finish the fourth article.

"Congratulations Tomas", Nikolai exclaimed, as soon as he saw me arrive. That afternoon, I finally managed to complete the fourth file and sent it to the relevant publication.

Having my work for the day completed, I called Herbert up, to share the latest news and above all, my enthusiasm with him. He always had a knack for sensing positive vibes, and had invited me to his house that evening, ostensibly to show me stuff he didn't need anymore, and could give us. Things were looking great, and I felt I had finally found the happiness I was looking for, but couldn't find, until now.

"Never love anyone who treats you like you're ordinary."

Oscar Wilde

IX. Engagement

Excited, but impatient for the end of Herbert's shift, I decided to take a stroll along the beach, through the Primorsky Park, and towards the Primorsky Boulevard, just to let off some steam. At 4:30 I texted him to pick me up by the park's main entrance, which Alexander did, in a short while. Herbert's house was fairly large. Five bedrooms, two baths, a large terrace, and even a small garden, all beautifully kept.

No sooner than we arrived, Herbert went to his large kitchen, opened the fridge, grabbed a bottle of tequila, and asked with a smile; "Want some?" How could I refuse a drink when I felt happy and was in a nice place like that? "Sure I'd like," I responded cheerfully. It came with an equally cold Baltica beer chaser. "Here's to your new place my friend", said Herbert, and knocked back the first tequila shot in an instant. A couple more rounds followed before he proceeded to show me the various items he offered to give me. "Fantastic, we'll have all of it if you don't mind. Thanks a lot." I said gratefully.

"What are friends for"? He asked with an impish spark in his eyes. Despite still being in his immaculate, stylish CEO attire, which he was gradually taking off piece by piece, this was no longer Herbert the Executive, but Herbert the Party Animal. The transformation was speedy, once he crossed the threshold of his house, and there weren't any witnesses around any longer. He'd only make an exception for Andrey, but no one else from his office. In his storage room, he then pointed out a kitchen table with chairs, an old but nice folding sofa, and even a used Philco washing machine. "Is this thing still working?" I asked curiously. "As well as my private part is!" He replied instantly, matter-of-factly, and looked me straight in the eye. Then, with a half-drunk expression on his face, he laughed out loud. Back in the living room, we settled into the comfortable, huge sofa again. He then called out to Svetlana, his trusted housekeeper in her late forties, to bring a pack of Cuban cigars. He passed me one, took one himself, served us

some more tequila, and we just kicked back cracking jokes, gossiping about people in town, etc. It just didn't get much better than that. All of a sudden, with a lit cigar still in his mouth, he picked up his iPhone, called Alexander up in a semi-drunk voice, and asked him to deliver the stuff to my new apartment on Saturday morning, with a little help from his friends, if need be. "What a guy!" I thought.

It was half-past ten on Saturday morning, when Angelina, Olga, and Andrey arrived, all together. They brought buckets, sponges, and detergent, and I don't know what else was with them. Furthermore, they brought a large, thick, folded foam mat, new beddings, some kitchenware, towels, soap, shampoo, and a number of other, smaller items. Basically, they brought everything that was needed for Angelina and me to spend our first night at the apartment together. A very nice gesture of them. I suppose both Andrey and Olga felt a sense of gratitude to us, for giving them the opportunity to meet each other, and this was their way of returning the favor. After a brief greeting and some unpacking, we got down to business. It goes without saying I hated this kind of work, but it had to be done, whether we liked it or not. The sooner, the better, we all agreed. Andrey and I focused on cleaning the living room and bedroom floors, while the girls took care of the kitchen and bathroom. With four people at it, the work progressed quickly, and in an hour, most of the apartment was clean, bar one of the bedrooms. Alexander showed up at noon, with all the stuff Herbert promised to give us in tow. We placed the table, chairs, and the Philco washing machine in the kitchen, the sofa in the living room, and the thick foam mat Andrey brought in one of the bedrooms. Now we only needed a fridge, some more stuff for the living room, and another bed for the second bedroom.

Since we were promised some more stuff from Jeremy and Sabrina, we decided to refrain from buying anything more, just in case. As of today, however, the apartment became habitable. Angelina's face brightened up when I presented her with the new set of keys. She didn't say anything, just pulled closer to me, and gave me that 'I-am-happy' type of smile, her trademark. A round of applause from Andrey and Olga followed. "Enjoy your new apartment guys, and best of luck," they said excitedly. They genuinely enjoyed helping us.

"Hope you guys help us too, when we get our own place", Olga quipped jokingly. By the time we were done with everything, it was almost evening, and I had ordered another takeaway pizza for the four of us. Then, while they all waited, I quickly went out to buy a bottle of chilled champagne and some more coke for the four of us to have a little celebratory dinner together, befitting the occasion. After our impromptu pizza dinner, Olga and Andrey proposed a toast with the Champagne. "This is to your new place, and our friendship". Before they left, Angelina and I warmly thanked them for their help and gifts.

Once again on our own, Angelina unpacked the new beddings and placed them on the thick foam mat, which we put in the bigger, nicer room, most likely our future master bedroom. The apartment was our pride and joy, a sign of things to come. Angelina then grabbed the unfinished champagne, took me by the hand, and led me to the living room sofa, where we continued sipping on it, till it was gone.

We just sat for a while, gently embracing, kissing, and talking. When we peeked out the window, it was already completely dark outside. The only things still visible were the flickering lights of distant fishing boats on the horizon. It was a magnificent view, straight from our own new apartment. After staring out the window into the distance for a few moments, we unpacked the remaining items, placed the toiletries in the bathroom, tidied up the kitchen, took a shower, grabbed our mobiles, and retreated to our new, barely furnished bedroom. With the window wide open, we could hear the occasional horn from passing ships, giving our place a romantic, holiday-like atmosphere. This was it. The symbolic importance of this moment was not lost on Angelina, and she tried her best to make it as

*romantic and pleasant as she could. I
reciprocated, and we spent the night kissing,
hugging, making love, and cuddling, till the
morning light.*

*After our first night, in our new apartment
together, we decided to have Sunday breakfast
at one of the cafes by the beach, a ten-minute
walk from our apartment.*

*Before we even set out, my phone rang. Jeremy
and Sabrina wanted to give us the things they
talked about. "Morning, do you guys want to
pick up the stuff Sabrina talked about"? Jeremy
asked. "Or, I can have someone from the
Agency bring it over if you want," he added.
"That would be great if you could," I replied
gratefully. "Sure, I'll send you a message when
they set out. Just don't stray too far from the
house, and have your mobile-ready", he added.
"Big thanks from both of us", said Angelina,
cutting in on the conversation. "We'll invite you
to the house warming party, once we get this
place up and running, probably next Saturday,"
I informed them casually. Angelina and I walked*

quickly toward the beach, sat down at the first café we saw, had a couple of sandwiches with coffee, and rushed back, just in case. The message came an hour later, and soon after, a couple of guys with a station wagon showed up. They brought the old fridge Sabrina mentioned, a small coffee table, and last but not least, a poster of a Cossack warrior on horseback with a sword. The guys placed the heavy fridge in the kitchen, and before they left, I slipped them a 400 Hryvna tip. The coffee table fitted nicely in front of Herbert's old sofa, and we placed the Cossack poster on the wall, opposite the sofa, for everyone to see. "What a nice gesture by Sabrina", Angelina remarked excitedly, and followed up by a couple of WhatsApp messages of gratitude. We were all set now! Just needed a microwave, a frypan, some rugs, and a few more minor things, which I could still afford. It had been a long day, and while it was nice and exciting, it was also tiring. Angelina had to go home to be ready for work the next morning, feed Tulko, and run some errands, while I had to go to my old apartment to fetch my stuff and give the owner a notice. We agreed to meet again on Tuesday evening, in our new apartment. In the meantime, I wanted to move all my things, buy a microwave, and some other small household items, and make the apartment ready for permanent habitation. When I walked past a stationery shop the next morning, I saw painting supplies. That's when I got the idea to turn the second, unused bedroom, into an art studio of sorts, for Angelina's work and hobbies.

"The equipment wasn't that expensive, and would surely please her," I assumed. Even though I wasn't quite sure whether she'd actually need all of this stuff, I wanted to please her and figured she could always use more equipment, even if she already had some. So I went ahead and got some canvas with a stand, a palette, acrylic paint, brushes, and some varnish, and placed all of it in the spare bedroom. I carefully placed the canvas on the stand, so that it would catch her eye immediately, upon entry. I used empty cardboard boxes covered with cloth as tables to

put her equipment on. Actually, the room ended up looking rather artistic, with the view of the sea in the background. "Perfect!" I breathed a sigh of relief. With the first task accomplished, I headed out to fetch the microwave. For convenience's sake, I ended up going to the Port City Mall, where I could check out other household items as well, and then relax with a cup of coffee at one of the cafes there. I bought the cheapest one I saw in the first shop, without much hesitation, or shopping around. "They all work the same anyways", I concluded. The other items I picked up were a small white rag carpet for the living room, and a black night lamp for our 'master bedroom'. Any kitchenware I'd buy later, I decided. On Tuesday morning, I went to a nearby supermarket, where I bought a non-stick frying pan, a cooking pot, a dozen eggs, bread, butter, ham, cheese, ketchup, and vegetables. Everything was now ready for Angelina to arrive. As agreed, she showed up at around six, dressed up in my favorite faded pink t-shirt, the faded tight blue jeans, and a black, casual jacket to keep her warm, with a large shopping bag in each hand. It was getting chilly in the evenings at the end of September, as the summer was drawing to a close, and people started dressing accordingly. She laid down her bags, gave me a nice kiss and we moved into the kitchen. We were at home and felt it. It was a strange sensation for both of us because neither one of us had experienced living together with a soul mate before. It took some getting used to. Angelina opened her shopping bags and pulled out a new wooden spoon, two kitchen knives, four sets of cutlery, cooking gloves, and a dishwashing detergent, among other things. It felt like a metamorphosis, which had just turned my new apartment into our new home. "Surprise! Can you close your eyes, follow me, and open them only after I tell you?" I asked unexpectedly. "You asked for it, you've got it", she giggled, closed her eyes, and followed me, led by the hand. Upon entry to the spare bedroom I said. "Open up!" Seeing her new art room, Angelina was pleased. She walked around, touched the canvas, smelled the acrylic paint, gently scraped the palette, and checked out the brushes, just like a pro. "How did you get this idea"? She asked curiously and happily, at the same time. As I was explaining she just smiled. Most likely, what she liked about it the most was the fact I was thinking about her, even when we were apart. "Hungry yet?" I asked. "Yes, I am. Do we have any food here"? She asked politely.

"I can cook scrambled eggs for you, just the way you cooked them for me at your place. Interested?" I suggested eagerly. For some reason, she liked my mannerism and the way I approached her. Suddenly, she started kissing me, touching me everywhere, embracing me. Naturally, I got excited and instinctively, we ended up in our master bedroom, on the foam mat, on the floor. Gradually, as we were kissing, we kept taking off each other's clothes. We ended up making wild love for at least an hour. Only after we were done, did she say; "Now, I'll prepare the eggs for both of us". I came to like her style. Angelina was quite impulsive and passionate when it came to lovemaking. She liked it best when it was not planned, nor *expected. And I could certainly live with that. It seemed we were not only a good match personality-wise, but we also got along well on the intimate side as well. She didn't mind doing the cooking either, as long as she believed I was not automatically expecting it from her, for being a woman, which I did not, and she sensed it. We still didn't have a cable TV or Wi-Fi. After dinner, I opened my laptop and we decided to watch 'The Mistress of Spice', a movie I had seen once before, liked, and had saved on my laptop. Angelina was quite taken by this movie, sympathetic to the main character, and asked for us to watch it together again sometime, a suggestion with which I had readily agreed. After such a lovely time together, we overslept. Fortunately, Angelina brought her work clothes with her and went to work straight from there.*

There were still a few things to repair, improved, and bought for this place, but it was already habitable, at least. I was trying to get some more sleep after Angelina left, but I just ended up tossing and turning, instead. My mind was wandering from one issue to another, and I found it difficult to set my priorities straight, at this point in time.

But certain things were clear. I needed to find out if I had already been paid, to prepare the apartment for our housewarming party, which was planned for Saturday. Every other issue could wait, for now.

During the rest of the week, together with Angelina, we cleaned, repaired, and fixed anything we could manage by ourselves, in order to welcome our friends, who had helped us so much.

On Friday evening we went to a supermarket and got some Jose Cuervo tequila, a must for Herbert, and a number of other drinks, including some Russian 'Champagne', so everyone could find something they fancied. We bought baguette bread, ham, cheese, eggs, mayonnaise, olives, and other stuff for hors-d'oeuvres. Angelina had texted everyone about the housewarming party a couple of days ago. Everyone, except Nikolai, who had to work, had agreed to come. On Saturday afternoon, the doorbell started ringing after five pm. Olga and Andrey showed up first, then Jeremy with Sabrina, thirty minutes later Herbert, and finally Jack, who had already appeared pretty plastered by the time he arrived."

"Nice pad", Sabrina said loudly, as she was checking it out. "Let me show you something", Angelina said excitedly, took her hand, and led her to the living room. Just as Sabrina noticed the Cossack poster on the wall, Angelina said; "Thanks so much for this poster. We love it and I am so proud of it. We always look at it when we sit down on the sofa here".

Herbert loved our location with the view, and commented, "Well done Tomas and Angelina, what a lovely apartment"! Most visitors had brought some extra drinks and snacks, so there was plenty to go around for everyone. Once everyone settled down a bit, we invited them to sit around the coffee table in the living room. Wherever they could sit, be it on the sofa, the chairs we had moved over from the kitchen, or the cushions we had put on the floor.

As soon as everyone was in position, Herbert exclaimed; "Here is a toast to Tomas and Angelina! We all wish them many happy years in this lovely, seaside apartment", and pulled out a bottle of Moët & Chandon from his bag. Clearly, he wanted to make this occasion special, and it didn't go unnoticed by Angelina and me. Everyone had a sip or two, and we all gradually sat back down around the old coffee table Herbert had given us. "What a familiar bunch of people", Jack quipped laughingly. He had a knack for saying things as they really were, and most people appreciated it. Indeed, we were basically the same bunch of people, who had been meeting at the Harbor Café for months, on a regular basis. Only Olga and Andrey were newcomers. But even they had already been well known, and well-liked, by all of us.

"I heard they sell nice engagement rings, just off Shevchenka Boulevard. When are you two getting engaged?" Jack quipped and laughed out loud again. He was drunk at this point and just didn't care. Under the influence, he was *usually just being honest, and said things that many had on their minds, but would not dare to say openly. Nevertheless, his comments immediately elicited a quick, surprised glance from Angelina. Having noticed that her cheeks had turned slightly red, I responded; "As soon as I get paid by my publication, should Angelina be interested." Suddenly, the ball was in Angelina's court, and she seemed to have been caught off guard. She glanced at me real quick, then at Olga, who then nodded her head so slightly that it was virtually unnoticeable to most guests, but not to me. I could read Olga's body language better than my friends. After a split second, Angelina gave us all a quick glance, and calmly said," I'd like to," with a broad smile. Everyone cheered and applauded her decision, but no one more so than Olga and Herbert. "Bravo Angelina", he stood up and exclaimed, clapping his hands. Giggling, good old Jack didn't even realize he had just fast-forwarded our relationship to a new level. It wasn't really important for Angelina or me, whether our relationship was made official or not. But since*

Jack had already suggested it, however clumsily, neither one of us saw any good reason to reject the idea, lest we offended each other needlessly. So we both simply went along with it. After all, I actually did have a good reason that our relationship is made more official. I wanted some certainty that it would be more permanent before I'd agree to make Angelina the official half owner of the new apartment. Otherwise, it made no difference to me. Angelina understood that our relationship was not based on whether it was made official or not. But she also knew it made a big difference when dealing with the authorities. And since she didn't want to complicate matters needlessly, she went along with the proposal without a fuss.

And what was meant to be strictly a housewarming party, had become an engagement party, at the same time. "Funny, how unpredictable life can become sometimes", I thought.

It was just another unexpected, but welcome development in my life in Mariupol. Once all the guests had left, Olga with Andrey helped us clean the place up. No sooner than the doors closed behind Olga and Andrey, and we were alone once again, Angelina came to me with that look in her eyes. I never exactly knew what she was thinking, I could only guess, but whatever it was, it was sweet and tantalizing. Just as she behaved in similar situations before, she embraced me tightly, gave me this magical deep kiss, and before I knew it, I was leading her to our foam mattress bed. She literally threw me down on it, laid on top of me and we made love. Except for this time, it felt even sweeter. An hour later, we were half asleep, in a cuddle. As we were lying there together, I thought to myself that whatever was meant by the phrase 'Being in Seventh Heaven,' must have applied to moments like these, right here, right now.

On Sunday morning, we woke up into a new phase in our relationship. However unimportant that 'engagement' idea may have sounded yesterday, it had been felt in our enhanced emotional as well as physical interaction last night.

We were glad the housewarming party went well last night, we were excited we were getting engaged, and we were happy we now had this new apartment near the beach to call home.

The only thing which bothered Angelina now was that Tulko had been left on his own for long periods of time, a practice he wasn't used to. "Just bring him over, I'd be happy to have him here with us," I suggested.

Angelina smiled, and warmly added; "I'll go home tonight, sort out my things, and I'll be back on Tuesday evening with Tulko, and some of my clothes." Now that we had a nice new place to live in, and a plan of action, we walked slowly through the refreshing Primorsky Park towards the beach, hand in hand.

You do not need a therapist if you own a motorcycle, any kind of motorcycle!

Dan Aykroyd

X. The Motorcycle.

Finally, Angelina and I had a place to call our own, were sort of engaged, and had met each other's parents, at least on WhatsApp.

Getting their tacit approvals meant we could now focus on continuing to build our future together.

Since our housewarming party unwittingly doubled as our engagement, I decided to buy two nice rings, and have Andrey with Olga be witnesses to exchanging our vows. But in order to do so, I needed my salary and kept checking my online account several times a day, to see if it had already been deposited.

It was due by Friday, and without it, I couldn't buy the rings, nor the other stuff. It finally came on Thursday from three publications, but not from the fourth one. Anyways, it was enough for the time being, so I immediately but secretly called Olga to help me select them.

She didn't see the need to throw another party to mark our engagement either and agreed our housewarming party had settled it.

Andrey was still busy at the port, so I met Olga alone, early in the afternoon. She worked as a hairdresser downtown, and it was relatively easy for her to sneak out. She took me to a small, modern jewelry shop, staffed by a couple of hip, young women.

Olga knew Angelina's taste better than I, so I essentially let her make the selection, for better or worse. I only knew which rings I didn't like, reducing myself to a spectator with veto power. After looking around and comparing for half an hour, we settled on a couple of simple-looking, matching, Solitaire-branded white gold rings. At 5400 Hryvna each, or about 180 Euro, they were not cheap, but they didn't break my piggy bank either. This had to be kept a secret, but we hatched a plan to surprise Angelina, sometime over the weekend. As agreed, all four of us met at the main entrance to the Primorsky Park on Saturday morning, ostensibly for lunch, and started walking, with Olga leading the way.

"What a nice day for a walk", Andrey said casually, knowing full well what the plan was. As we were approaching the bench area where Angelina and I had sat on our first date, Olga pretended her legs started hurting, walked toward the bench I pinpointed to her earlier, sat down, and made herself comfortable.

With an expression of surprise on her face, Angelina looked at me, and said; "Isn't this the bench we sat on that night?" "It sure is, and I'd like to show you something. Could you please close your eyes for a moment?" I requested unexpectedly.

Angelina sensed we had a trick up our sleeve, but obliged. Olga then quickly opened the black jewelry box and started pushing the ring up Angelina's finger. "Open up now!" Olga said excitedly. "Wow", was all that Angelina could muster at that moment. Olga then quickly placed the other ring on my finger, and requested politely; "Now, give each other a kiss, then promise you will love and support each other till the end of time". We happily obliged and did the honors one after another.

Despite the fact Angelina knew we made a promise to get engaged, she simply had not expected it here, and now. Once she regained her composure, she thanked all three of us for this wonderful surprise; "I am so happy you guys did this for me, and of all places, right here. I will never forget it!" "Neither will I", I promptly added eagerly. We gave each other another kiss and held each other tight for a few moments. "The rings are so beautiful. How did you find them, Tomas?" Angelina asked curiously. "Actually, Olga helped me with it," I admitted sheepishly.

With our surprise engagement ceremony behind us, we proceeded to walk toward the beach and ended up walking all the way to the end of the pontoon bridge, the sea breeze blowing in our hair. "So, when will you two get engaged?" Angelina asked Andrey teasingly. Just as Jack's question caught me by surprise at the housewarming party, it caught both Andrey and Olga by surprise in equal measure. They looked at each other for a split second, with smiles on their faces, but didn't manage to utter a word. It undoubtedly planted seeds in their heads, but it had caught them both off guard. Only their body language provided some hints. Olga's piercing, green eyes began to radiate like an x-ray machine, while Andrey struggled to find an appropriate response, short of an outright offer.

Having noticed the unease Angelina's innocent but naughty joke brought about, I quickly tried *to change the subject." I wonder how far it is from Mariupol to Batumi. Anyone knows?" "It only takes an hour by plane, so it should be some 800 kilometers", Angelina speculated. "Close guess Angelina," I commanded her. "Anyone else would like to guess?" I asked again." "Just under 700 km", Andrey said confidently. "Wow, an excellent guess! How did you know?" I asked in amazement. "Anyone who works at the Port of Mariupol can tell you", Andrey replied boldly, with a smile.*

The only reason I knew was that I looked it up online, out of sheer curiosity, in case we went to visit Angelina's mom there.

After sitting and chatting for almost an hour on the edge of the bridge I stood up and asked. "Anyone up for a drink at Barbaris? My treat. Today is a very special day." The offer was quickly accepted by all, especially so by Angelina, and off we went. It only took about ten minutes on foot from the pontoon bridge. The location of all the places we went to today had special meaning for both Angelina and me.

We met at the Barbaris, and had our first date on that park bench. I talked to Angelina's mom in that park, and Angelina talked to my folks on the pontoon bridge. We now even lived in this fancy area. So I thought a few drinks at Barbaris, on the day of our engagement, would put it all in the right perspective. We spent a couple of hours chatting, dancing, and dining there. Dinner was served on the terrace, against the backdrop of the calm sea. Even though it ended up costing me almost 2000 Hryvna, it was worth every penny, on such a special occasion. Impressed and enthused by the developments in our relationship, Andrey and Olga invited us to dinner the next weekend. We returned home tired, but relaxed, happy, and cheerful.

Tulko greeted us with his typical 'zdravstvuj' shrieks, flying from one end of the hallway to the other, eventually landing on Angelina's head. Bringing him over had turned our new apartment into a home, and it only took him a few hours to get used to it. As we sat around the kitchen table, feeding him pieces of apple and carrot, I noticed Angelina kept sporadically glancing at the new ring. As low-key as the unofficial 'park engagement ceremony' may have been, it seemed to have a profound, steadying effect on both of us. Later that night, while drinking a beer in the kitchen, I asked Angelina curiously; "I heard someone is selling an older, 2002 Honda Trans Alp motorcycle. Do you think I should check it out?" "Absolutely, I'd love that! Remember, we talked about it that night in the park". Angelina reminded me excitedly. "How could I forget"? I calmly reassured her. Emboldened by our strong bond, I was no longer afraid to make an additional, relatively small investment. Especially when I knew how handily it would come in. "I'm going to check it out on Monday, first thing in the morning," I told her. Having been told what a big fan of motorcycles I was, Andrey had found out that some chap in town was selling his bike. So, on Monday morning, Angelina and I took a cab, we dropped her off at the school, and I continued to this place, to check the bike out. The chap pulled it out of an old, rusty metal cage, commonly referred to as a garage in this part of the world, for me to see. It looked somewhat beat up here and there, scraped on the right side, with the right rearview mirror missing. Other than that, it still seemed in pretty good shape. The fact he had taken a dive on the right side was clear for all to see, but it didn't mean there had to be real damage. He started it up with jump-start cables connected to his car's battery. The engine sounded pretty normal, and I figured a new battery might be all that's really needed for now. It seemed the dive didn't cause any damage to the engine, and the right side panels could easily be smoothed out at anybody's shop, while the right mirror could easily be replaced, even if it came from another type of motorcycle.

When I test-rode it around the block, I realized it was in fairly good running order. It only needed a new clutch cable, new air filter, new chain, and possibly a few additional, minor things. Naturally, it also needed a general tune-up. Most importantly, all the motorcycle really needed were a few, relatively minor, and inexpensive things. While they all needed to be done as soon as possible, they weren't that expensive, nor too difficult for any self-respecting mechanic to do, to my big relief. I liked it, wanted it, but tried not to show it. "Not bad, but it needs some bodywork, parts replacements, and a thorough service," I said after the ride, matter-of-factly. While the asking price was 55.000 Hryvna, I wasn't prepared to pay the full amount. "Would you settle for 40.000 Hryvna?" I tried to bargain reasonably. We ended up agreeing on 45.000. Despite the fact I didn't show it, I was as excited as a little kid. Life would now get a lot nicer, and easier for us. That much was certain. I rode it to the first café along the way, ordered a double espresso with milk, and called Herbert up. I had to spill the beans, and asked if he knew of any reputable repair shop in town. As expected, he was excited to hear the news. In his office, he had to talk quietly, but I could sense his excitement. "I'll see what I can find out. Give me ten minutes", he said enthusiastically and hung up. The phone rang in a couple of minutes, and he went; "The nearest Honda dealer is in Dnipro, but there is a good repair shop right here in town, called Xamyt Custom, on Olympijska St, 77. How bad are the repairs you need?" He asked anxiously. "It runs for now, but I'll definitely need to get it into a repair shop as soon as possible. I'll try the Xamyt Custom shop right now," I said impatiently. And off I went. The chaps at the shop checked it out and pretty much confirmed the same things I expected. They could replace the battery, the chain, and the mirror right now. They could also change the oil, but the air filter and the bodywork only later. Since these were the most pressing issues the bike needed, I agreed, and they got to work. It went without saying I considered myself lucky they could do all those things right away. This meant I could start riding immediately and take Angelina for the promised ride still today, after school. Effectively, I could now start using the bike on a daily basis, while the weather was still relatively warm. I would only need to get the registration paperwork sorted, a mere formality. At the end of the day, it would also enable me to do my job as a journalist more easily, and better, while having fun at the same time. Furthermore, it would enable me to drive Angelina around, pick her up from school, go shopping, and take trips out of town together. Just the way Angelina imagined it that night, on our first date. Overcome by excitement, I could not resist showing it to Angelina straight on the way from the repair shop. I pulled up in front of the school, parked the bike in front of the entrance on the sidewalk, got up, and asked the guard to let me in.

Because he had seen me dropping Angelina off by taxi a few times before, he let me in. As I was approaching Angelina's classroom, I could hear her Grade-1 kids singing. I waited till they had finished, then knocked on the door. One of the kids came up to open, and upon seeing me, called Angelina over. Very surprised to see me, she invited me into the class, to the surprise of the kids. She introduced me as her fiancée. "Hello class, how are you today"? I greeted the kids enthusiastically, in English. "I am fine thank you", they responded cheerfully, showing off their limited English skills boldly. They were a bunch of friendly, lovely kids. Not only did they like Angelina the teacher, they also seemed to have taken to me. Running toward me, they started embracing me, holding on to my pants and shirt.

Angelina must have told them something nice about me, I figured. "What a surprise", Angelina whispered. "I am happy to see that the kids like you and that you like them too. But I suspect the main reason you came is the bike, right"? She said excitedly, looking me in the eye.

"I've got it right outside the school, take a look!" I told her impatiently. She went straight over to the window, kids in tow, and upon seeing it, said with enthusiasm; "Wow, fantastic! Can't wait to take a ride".

"I'll pick you up at four-thirty, right outside the entrance". I declared triumphantly, as I was leaving the class. "Bye Mr. Tomas, the kids said in unison and went back to cutting some colored paper and singing.

A big selling point was that the bike already had a rear rack mounted on it. A top box and side boxes could easily be attached to it for longer trips, as well as for shopping. I only needed to invest some three hundred euros more, including repairs, to make it a perfectly functioning, good-looking machine. It never felt so easy moving around Mariupol, as it felt now. I rode along Shevchenko and Primorsky Boulevards, down near the port, and all the way beyond the Azovstal Metallurgic Plant, broadening my horizons and enhancing my knowledge of the town almost instantly.

Motorbikes always added another dimension to life anywhere, at least for me. A lot easier to get around on than in cars, in any city, or on terrain.

A dual-purpose adventure bike such as this was the perfect machine for exploring this part of Ukraine, and beyond. Impatient till Angelina finished her work, I cruised to the western part of town, in the direction of Dnipro, just to kill some time. Finally, the time was right to fetch Angelina, and I sped toward the school. As soon as she saw me, she walked over, kissed me, and jumped right behind me. She held me tight, just the way she said she would, on that park bench at night, on our first date. "I love the bike! Well done. What are you waiting for"? She asked eagerly, from behind. I reached into my backpack, pulled out the new, purple helmet I had bought for her, and placed her bag between the two of us. No sooner than she put her helmet on, we sped off. To maximize the ride's enjoyment, I took the road out of town, leading toward Dnipro again, with less traffic on it. Once out of the city limits, I twisted the throttle a bit harder, to show Angelina what the bike could do. Being a v-twin, the bike just purred and leaped forward, eliciting excitement in Angelina. "Oh, wow, amazing ride", she shouted through her helmet visor and squeezed me even tighter. We went on for some ten more minutes, reaching speeds of over 170 km/h, before I slowed down, and turned around. When we arrived at our apartment complex and got off the bike, Angelina was absolutely overjoyed. So were the kids in the playground, who saw us, and came running towards us, to satisfy their curiosity. "I am so glad we have this bike", Angelina said excitedly, touching the bike's gas tank with one hand, and holding her helmet with the other. "I loved the ride, and am so happy that you fulfilled your promise from our first date, to take me for a ride one day", she confided in me sweetly. "The pleasure is all mine," I replied happily. "We'll do it many more times, I assure you", I added casually. But I never realized just how much Angelina would enjoy riding this thing. More than I had expected, and that was a good thing. This ride electrified her, and before we went upstairs, she told the kids to stay away from the bike, in order not to damage it, by accident. The kids promised, but when we looked out the window, they were climbing all over it, unable to resist the temptation. And not only the boys, but the girls too, in an equal measure! Concerns about the bike's safety prompted Angelina to shout something at the kids from our window. She shouted either in Ukrainian, or in Russian, and whatever she may have said, the kids left the bike alone, upon hearing it. Once the bike safety issue had been resolved, Angelina came straight to me, grabbed me by the waist, and started kissing me passionately. I never saw her as electrified, as she was today. Affectionate, passionate, even outright wild. Naturally, I only welcomed her initiative with open arms. In no time, we were on the living room sofa, making love. I always suspected most young women liked rides on big motorcycles, but I never expected Angelina would respond quite like this. It seemed to have released the devil inside of her! However, after today's exciting ride, followed by wild hanky-panky, and a busy day at school, she was exhausted. Because she still needed to do some work preparation, I decided to show the bike off to some friends. Today being a Monday, it was unlikely there would be anyone to show the bike to at the Café. Even Nikolai wasn't often there on Mondays. So I decided to take a ride near Herbert's house, and call him from there. Fortunately for me, he wasn't particularly busy, and without much fuss, asked me to stop by his house with the bike. "You son of a gun, you did it"! He exclaimed cheerfully, upon seeing the bike. "You've got to let me take it for a spin, just around the corner here", he demanded. "Go for it," I said hurriedly and passed him the keys. Being a wild character as he was, Herbert revved it up, burning the rear tire in the process, then sped off around the corner. A couple of minutes later he showed up again, still in one piece, with bulging eyes, and a wide smile. "Loved it", he said triumphantly. "It's a good machine, for a good price", he remarked. I knew he would like it. He was a wild, unrestrained man in his private life, drawn to any adventure like a moth to a flame.

So much so, that I sometimes wondered whether his CEO position was merely his alter ego. "I got to get me one of these", he murmured to himself, as he was getting off the bike. We stood around the bike for a while, checking it out. I didn't even go inside his house this evening. I just wanted to show it off, and *hear someone's opinion. Herbert did just that. Satisfied, I suggested that we meet tomorrow at the café, if possible. He accepted, and I rode back home. Inside the apartment, all the lights had already been turned off. Exhausted by the events of the day, Angelina had gone to bed. Only Tulko still greeted me with his semi-intelligible, sleepy small talk, perched upon a branch we found for him at the park, and affixed high up, near the kitchen window. It became his favorite hangout, ever since.*

He started hopping around and talking when he saw me. I turned on the kitchen light, chopped up a small piece of apple, and sat down at the table. In no time, Tulko started descending down to the table by way of the curtains, chopping them up here and there in the process. He then hopped around the table and started taking bites off the apple. Somehow, I didn't feel sleepy yet. I quietly opened the bedroom door and saw Angelina spread across the whole foam mattress, soundly asleep. I quietly returned to the kitchen to chill out some more. Because of the bike, I was too excited to sleep. So I opened a can of Baltika beer, and relaxed. With Tulko by my side, Angelina in bed, and the bike parked down below, it really felt like being at home now. I had realized I was happy, through and through. What an amazing feeling it was! About twenty minutes later, a sleepy Angelina emerged from the bedroom, dressed in a see-through nightgown, with a part of her breast exposed. She walked up to me, put her arms around me from behind, placed her cheek against mine, and just stood there, yawning. It was perhaps her unspoken invitation for me to come and join her in the bedroom. She looked so cute. I pulled her beside me, lifted her up, and placed her on my lap. We were sitting there for a few minutes cuddling, just like that, without anything being said. I ran my fingers through her disheveled, long, blond hair, over and over. She started falling asleep again, leaning against me, like a little girl. I didn't want to interrupt her comfortable, sleepy position, and continued sitting there for a good thirty minutes, just like that. By seeing her exposed legs and breast, and touching her hair and cheeks, I was starting to get turned on, even excited. I started touching her legs, kissing her breast and cheeks. Gradually, she started kissing me back. At this point, I stood up and carried her to bed. We made love again, and then fell asleep together. We didn't even hear the phone alarm in the morning and got up late. It was almost nine am when we woke up, and Angelina was supposed to be at school before nine, each morning. She jumped in the shower real quick, then grabbed her things, and I drove her to school without even getting washed up myself. Due to my quick, creative riding, she ended up being only twenty minutes late, fortunately. That afternoon I picked her up from school again, and we rode to the Harbor Café together. It was so much more fun riding the bike than going by taxis or buses, and a lot cheaper too. We started going places more frequently than before, as a result. The bike soon became an inseparable part of our lives.

Not many ex-pats were usually there on Tuesdays, but after hearing about my new bike, a few of them showed up. Jeremy and Sabrina were already having dinner, while Jack was having an intense chat with Nikolai at the bar. Andrey and Olga were helping Natalia with something in the kitchen. Herbert had been busy with some unfinished tasks at the office, and could not make it today. It was just as well, as far as I was concerned, because he had already seen the bike the night before. Andrey finally emerged from the kitchen and saw the bike for the first time. "Great bike", he said excitedly.

Proud to be the one who had found the seller, he wanted to test ride it, even though he had never ridden a big motorcycle before. He did manage to spin it around the parking lot real slow, while Olga, who just came from the kitchen, nervously looked on. When he was getting off of it, he let go of the handlebars too soon, and nearly dropped the damn thing on my foot. Fortunately, we managed to stabilize it fell all the way. Despite his obvious blunder, but enthused by the bike, he said haltingly; "I must get one of these things".

Jack, Jeremy, and Nikolai were not really interested in bikes, but they did agree it was convenient, and loads of fun. Only Herbert was a true motorcycle enthusiast, who had already shown his passion, and demonstrated he could ride well.

Anxiety is the hand maiden of creativity.

T. S. Eliot

XI. The Troop Buildup

Sitting at the café, Sabrina and Angelina were like old buddies. With Olga by their side today, the trio had a lot to tell each other, chatting *happily amongst themselves, for most of the evening. It was late October now, and while the girls were busy chatting, Jack gathered us guys around one side of the table, to tell us he was concerned about the situation on the Russian side of the border. Apparently, a substantial buildup of Russian armored forces, near the border with eastern Ukraine, had been observed. "It's probably just an intimidation tactic", Jeremy remarked cautiously. "Or maybe they are just trying to boost the morale of the separatists," I added. "This is highly unusual", Nikolai said, with a surprised look on his face. While we were all surprised, even concerned, we didn't let the news spoil our regular, enlightened evening chat, complete with drinks, snacks, and all. We simply thought it didn't amount to much. Even Jack himself didn't think any danger was imminent. Then, I suddenly remembered, that one of the magazines I was writing for, had recently asked me to write a piece on the situation at the border. Remembering this, I asked Jack if he could tell me some more stuff about this issue, in order for me to write a report. "It's classified, you know," he cautioned me, while he downed another Scotch on the rocks. "I know, I know, just give me some bits and pieces. I need to make a living man," I pushed him persistently... "Ok, I'll think of something", he answered reluctantly. Being a ranking ex SAS officer in charge of training the Ukrainian special forces, he had extensive knowledge of the situation. "Do you think we are now in any danger here because of the buildup?" people asked nervously. "Not really, but it is a cause for concern, nevertheless", he elaborated. The next morning, after dropping Angelina off at school, I headed to his special-forces training ground. Jack had arranged for me to be let in at the gate, and a soldier guided me to the grounds. There, I saw soldiers, heavily armed with automatic assault weapons, bazookas, ammunition straps, and hand grenades. They were dressed in olive green and black camouflage uniforms, their faces painted black, climbing over barriers, jumping over obstacles, crawling under spiked wires, and randomly firing at practice targets. They all looked intimidating, to say the least, and I was sure they could destroy any enemy if put to the task. With gunfire resonating throughout the grounds, and smoke billowing in all directions, Jack emerged from his command bunker. Clearly in his element, dressed in camouflage fatigues, wearing a green beret, dark shades, a sidearm holster filled with a pistol, and a pair of binoculars hanging around his neck, he came to show me around the training grounds. It felt more like being on a movie set of Arnold Schwarzenegger's 'Commando', than at a real training ground. "Good to see you, Tomas, enjoy the show! Just don't write the true location of these grounds, or any real names of anyone involved in this, to the papers please! Deal?" He asked cautiously. "Deal," I responded. We walked around the grounds, while Jack was explaining the various activities, and their purposes, and enlightened me about some of the equipment. It was a real eye-opener for me, I must admit. Needless to say, it sent chills down my spine, just wondering what all that equipment and training was needed for. It appeared as if they were getting ready for all hell breaking loose! But I hoped, and believed, like everyone else, it would never come to that. Afterward, I sent a long report to my publication, which was well-received, and well paid too. So much so, that pretty soon, I got additional requests to write more reports on related issues. With such financial incentives, I decided to take a ride towards the line of control, the unofficial border between Ukraine and the Separatists, despite Angelina's objections. "You are pushing your luck. What if they detain you there? Or even shoot you? Are you out of your mind"? Angelina protested. "Don't worry, I'll be careful, and won't go too far," I assured her. "Do you know how much they want to pay me for this report?" I reminded her haltingly but to no avail. "I don't care how much. It's not worth the danger, can't you see"? She replied angrily and was adamant that I do not go there.*

So, I hatched a sneaky little plan, to go there secretly. I dropped her off at school on

Thursday, and after that, I proceeded on the road towards Novoazovsk, a city located completely inside the separatist region. The line of control wasn't that far out of town, a mere ten-mile ride from Mariupol. I heard all about it but had never actually been there. As I was getting nearer, I had been stopped at the first checkpoint. They looked dead serious, asked me numerous questions, and treated me with a degree of suspicion. Slightly worried, but undeterred, I had duly explained that I was a free-lance reporter, and wanted to write a story about the situation at the border for my employer, a news publication. But despite my best efforts, they told me I could go no further. At a loss and out of desperation, I picked up my mobile and called Jack. I told him I was on a report mission, and they didn't want to let me go even as far as the Ukrainian part of the border. Annoyed but cooperative, Jack asked me to hold on a minute. In a short while, he came back on the line and asked me to pass the phone to one of the soldiers at the checkpoint, which I did. After exchanging several sentences with Jack, the soldier returned my phone and waved me on. Gratefully, I said a few words of kindness to Jack, and rode on, till I reached the Ukrainian part of the border. The soldiers there already knew I was coming, and gave me a mini-tour of the area, explaining the situation, as I had never heard it before. Only then did I realize, just how important Jack was to the local military authorities. Without his help, I would stand no chance of being let through, let alone being guided around the border area, like a tourist on an all-inclusive package tour. Jack and I decided to keep this a secret, especially from Angelina, and from all the other friends by default, lest she found out.

The trip was a real eye-opener for me. I always knew there was a tense situation out there, but had been told it was peaceful and safe, which it was. Yet despite the relative calm, seeing so many heavily armored vehicles, artillery pieces, and even tanks, was a sobering experience, if not a frightening one. Just as the report before it, it was a good sell in Europe, and I got decent money for it. We needed the money, for all sorts of things. Nevertheless, I continued to keep it a secret from Angelina, rather than running the gauntlet of her anger, possibly damaging our relationship in the process. Having written these two reports, I decided to give this topic a rest, at least for now, despite the good payoffs. Sticking my nose into these matters, I concluded, might not only get me in trouble but undermine our nice relationship, which was of far greater importance to me.

Armed with two fat, but secret paychecks, I decided to buy some more art-related equipment for Angelina, so she could enjoy her favorite pastime, and paint over the weekend. On Friday afternoon, before picking her up, I stopped by one of the bike shops to see whether they had some motorcycle gear and clothing. They did, and I ended up buying myself a warm riding jacket, complete with pants. It was important to wear such gear, in case we took a dive, and also because winter was just around the corner. I bought a large, forty-liter GIVI top box, along with a couple of matching, thirty-five-liter side boxes, which I then locked onto the rear rack. The plan was to bring Angelina here on Saturday morning and let her select her bike clothing by herself. On the way to pick her up from school, I stopped by a big stationery shop, and picked up several large sketching papers, a couple of hard as well as soft sketching pencils,

and a few more color paints. Unfortunately, some of the stuff didn't fit into the top box, and protruded from my backpack, potentially ruining the surprise, meant for the home unpacking. "Wow, you bought all this for me"? Angelina asked assuredly, as soon as she approached the bike. "You bet I did," I responded without letting my disappointment show and stole a quick kiss. As we were riding past the clock tower, Angelina asked me to stop. She carefully observed it, measured it with her eyes, and then said, "Let's go". After dinner, which I prepared that evening, she closed herself off in the spare bedroom and didn't emerge for a couple of hours. Then she opened the door and called me in. "I don't believe this!" I said upon entering the room. "Amazing, you *did this just now?" I asked in disbelief. She just smiled and presented me with a painting. "It's for you", she added. It was a supersized Tulko, in his true blue, black and white colors. It looked so real, that I was flabbergasted. I guess I had not realized what a great artist Angelina truly was, until now. "' I'll have it framed, and we'll put it on our living room wall, opposite the Cossack, what do you say?" I asked enthusiastically. Angelina agreed, and the next day, before she returned from school, I had it framed and hung it up. It livened up our living room and made Angelina feel proud. On the heels of that success, on Saturday morning, we set out to go to the clock tower.*

Before we got there, though, I made a detour to the bike shop, for Angelina to select her own riding gear. After all, we wanted to keep riding through the winter, and the cold weather was just around the corner now. Since I had already bought mine, and also had a pair of very strong shoes and gloves suitable for riding, it was her turn. After carefully looking through, and trying on a number of items, she settled for a new, warm, waterproof, black and white RSA kit, complete with pants, gloves, and riding shoes. Though the whole package set me back over three hundred euros, I didn't mind. It was money well spent, as far as I was concerned. Besides, Angelina looked so good in that gear, that I couldn't wait for our first cold-weather trip.

Now that we were all set for winter riding, we proceeded toward the clock tower. There, we parked the bike on a sidewalk, under our watchful eyes, and sat on the curb. Angelina pulled out her sketch papers and started drawing. She was in her element.

First, she made a large sketch of the tower, using her new sketch paper and pencils. Then she told me confidently. "Take a forty-five-minute ride if you like, and when you come back, the color painting will be finished." Even though I didn't mind watching her while she painted, I obliged. When I came back an hour later, not only was she munching on large ice cream at a nearby kiosk, but she had painted *the whole tower, like a pro. It looked so real, that I had it framed, and put it up in our hallway. Her evident talent prompted me to start taking photos of all her paintings, which I then sent to my family, as well as friends. Some of them were so impressed, that they had asked Angelina to make a painting, or a sketch, just for them. Not that Angelina didn't want to do it. She enjoyed painting a lot, but we also realized we could not refuse people, who had helped us before.*

So, we got down to business. It wasn't a big deal for Angelina. We were asked for a couple of paintings for our best friends. In order to help remedy the situation I had created, by sending the pictures around, I had become Angelina's 'assistant'. Driving her around, carrying, packing, unpacking, and cleaning her painting equipment, as needed. Now that we had an apartment in such a great location, we simply walked down to the beach, set all our gear up, and Angelina proceeded to paint the pontoon bridge, to give to Sabrina and Jeremy as a gift.

I observed keenly, as Angelina was painting the outlines. She kept adding various strokes, colors, and lines until it all began to resemble the bridge. It was an amazing experience for me to watch her paint. I was attracted both to her work, and to her as a person. That's why I didn't mind hanging around, even when it took some time. This weekend was still relatively warm, so hanging out at the beach was pleasant anyways. This pontoon bridge painting was the first one Angelina gave away as a gift. The recipients were certainly well deserving of it, and Jeremy had put it up in the living room of their spacious apartment, for all to see.

Next in line, asking for a picture, was Herbert. There was absolutely no way we could say no to him, after everything he had done for us. Duly, Angelina made her best effort to please him. She gifted him a large, beautiful, black and white sketch of the Mariupol Cathedral of the Archangel Michael. Not that there was anything wrong with her selection. Herbert was a very good person, and few could match his many good deeds.

Despite all that, however, I just couldn't reconcile this holy image with Herbert's flamboyance, wild partying, and unorthodox ways, try as I might.

Suspecting some sort of prank, I carefully asked Angelina, whether she selected this type of picture for Herbert just for fun, or seriously. Not getting my point, she asked curiously; "What do you mean? I don't understand your question."

Angelina, rather innocently, had not connected all the dots. As far as she was concerned, Herbert might as well be a saint. While both of us held him in high esteem, we did so for slightly different reasons, and it showed.

I certainly didn't want to change her perception of him, so I just joked around, that gifting him that picture was like gifting the 'Devil Incarnate' the Holy Cross.

She did like the joke but didn't fully grasp the subtle punchline. Clearly, she saw him in a slightly different light, and for all intents and purposes, that was a good thing.

Interestingly, she always giggled, whenever I mentioned it. With Herbert's claim out of the way, next on 'the waiting list' was Nikolai, who wanted to hang one of her paintings at the Harbor Café, for good luck.

Knowing he was an ex-soldier, Angelina decided to sketch a picture of the old Cossack fortress - The Zaporozhian Sich for him. She based the sketch on a picture from a brochure we got on our visit there. On our next visit to the Harbor Café, she presented him with the framed sketch, which he then proudly placed above the bar area, for all to see. Nikolai was so fond of the picture, he decided to serve us free meals that night. Angelina did not forget Olga with Andrey either. In order to help cement their relationship, Angelina made a large color painting, depicting the silhouettes of two lovers on a tropical island. While the painting turned out nice, it just wasn't my cup of tea, but I never said anything. Besides, she knew Olga a lot better than I did, so who was I to tell her what to paint?

After that, without telling me, Angelina sketched the outline of the city of Mariupol. It was large and so impressive, that I wanted to hang it in the hallway of our apartment, until she told me it was a gift for my parents, to be presented on our planned visit, in June.

The best holiday I ever had was the first one I went on without my parents.

Joe Elliott

XII. The Holidays

The weather wasn't getting any warmer, and it was becoming much less comfortable to do artwork outside. Angelina started painting less frequently, and when she did paint, it was mostly from the comforts of our home. Taking a small break from it wouldn't do her any harm, as she readily admitted, and would give her more time to catch up on long-neglected duties elsewhere. Besides, Christmas was nearly here and she'd be busy with that pretty soon. There were also other things to do for her, like visiting her grandparents one of these days, time permitting. A trip she wanted me to join her on.

Since this was to be our first Christmas together as a couple, both of us wanted to make sure the other felt as comfortable and happy, as possible.

While Ukraine officially switched from celebrating Christmas Day from January 7th to December 25th only in 2017, it meant many, if not most, Ukrainians would still celebrate the Orthodox version of it. Mindful of that, the switch still made the holiday celebration more convenient for us, as a mixed couple. It was a subtle indication of the fact that Ukraine was moving closer to the West, not only politically or economically, but also culturally. It wasn't that important to me what religion Angelina subscribed to, but celebrating Christmas together, along the same lines, and on the same day, surely made life easier for both of us.

There were now only a couple of days left to prepare for it, so we divided up the tasks. I was to fetch the tree somewhere, help out with grocery shopping, and clean, while Angelina would get the decorations, cook the meals, and bake some pastries.

Dutifully, I set out to search for the tree on the bike, as usual. Fortunately for me, the weather wasn't too cold in wintertime in Mariupol, according to Herbert, who had spent the last Christmas here. Apparently, the city was being warmed by the sea, and as a result, the roads were almost always passable, with the snow melting on them almost as soon as it fell. This meant we could basically use the bike throughout the winter, but only for short rides. Riding longer in the cold air just wasn't enjoyable, even if technically possible. For getting around the town, however, the bike was quick, convenient, and cheap. So I saddled up, cruised around for a bit, and pretty soon, I saw a stand selling Christmas trees, not that far from Primorsky Boulevard. In order to make our first Christmas together special, and impress

Angelina, I bought one of the biggest and nicest pine trees they had. Having bought the stand already, I had it delivered to our apartment. It was so huge, that they had to cut it down by about 50 cm. Angelina wasn't home when they brought it, so I decided to surprise her a bit, and have the tree standing in the middle of the living room, for when she comes. "That's so huge and very nice", she said admiringly, as soon as she saw it. "Smells nice too", she added sweetly, as she was walking around it, smelling and touching it, here and there. "Look what I've got!" she then said, showing me the various Christmas decorations she pulled out of the bag.

"This I got from mom's apartment, and that I bought", she said matter-of-factly, as she was showing me the Christmas lights, various glass balls, a rubber spider web, and a tree topper. We spent the whole evening decorating it, and it turned out to look gorgeous. Excited like a couple of school kids starting their vacations, we sat on the sofa, kept looking at it, and made various suggestions. The next day being Christmas Eve, we both had lots of things to

take care of. The 25th was an official holiday in Ukraine now, but Angelina and the kids got the 24th off as well. I knew she would still have time to buy more stuff if she needed to. We both needed some time to ourselves to do things, so we went our separate ways, early in the morning. I always enjoyed exchanging presents but hated the selection process. Doing it for Angelina, however, was a rare exception. I set out early, and by nine am, I was up and about. "Should I buy her some jewelry? More art equipment? Clothes"? I had no idea, and it was eating me up. Unable to make a sound decision, I decided to call Olga, but there was no answer. So, I decided to get more adventurous and called Herbert. He never disappointed and advised me to buy her some Channel perfume with a make-up kit. "Excellent idea!" I thanked him, and off I went. Once in the bag, I decided to buy her one more item, selected strictly by myself, just to prove a point. In the absence of any better ideas, I decided to go to the 'sure bet' bike shop again. "There, I'll find something she might find handy," I reasoned. Then I saw it.

A beautiful, long, warm riding coat, perfect for even longer winter rides. "Warmer and longer than the one she had selected by herself, she would probably find it useful," I thought. What better present to give a girl who enjoyed riding so much, and whom I loved dearly? "That's the right choice," I thought, and bought her the W-TEC Touring Jacket. It was three-layered, relatively long, armored, and rainproof. "This would make even longer winter rides comfortable, and she would probably welcome it," I figured. I went ahead and bought it, then had both items gift-wrapped at a department store. I was all set. When I got back that evening, Angelina was in the kitchen, baking something delicious, from which the smell of cinnamon emanated throughout the apartment.

I tried to hide the gifts real quick, but before I managed to tell her not to look, she poked her head through the hallway door and saw them. Recognizing her mistake, she quickly disappeared back into the kitchen. We were planning to place all the gifts under the tree early morning, on Christmas Day.

Due to the fact that neither Angelina nor I had our closest family members around, we planned to make WhatsApp calls to both our families, as well as to a select group of friends on Christmas Day, sometimes after lunch. Furthermore, we had invited Olga and Andrey to stop by in the evening. As a sign of close friendship between Angelina and Olga, Angelina even allowed her to 'spend some time at her family apartment along with Andrey, and save them money for hotels, where they otherwise had to go for their intimate encounters. Needless to say, she had full trust in Olga to keep the place clean and tidy. It turned out Angelina had already picked up gifts for them, sparing me the hassle.

On Christmas Day we woke up late, cuddling lazily, and taking our time. Yesterday had been a hectic day, and we needed the extra rest. Each of us had already placed our gifts under the tree late last night when the other one wasn't looking. There was no hurry now. Eventually, we slowly crawled out of bed, took showers, and decided to prepare breakfast. It wasn't going to be a special Christmas breakfast though. Just our usual scrambled eggs, coffee, or tea. This morning, I'd be the one to prepare it, to give Angelina a much-needed break. Making eggs in the morning was an activity I enjoyed anyways or at least didn't mind. I made coffee, toasted four slices of bread, put some butter on them, and breakfast was served. Putting some Heinz ketchup on the eggs was a must, as far as I was concerned, and even Angelina got hooked on it. We took our time eating, sipping coffee, chatting, touching, and even kissing. Tulko, who would not miss an opportunity to grab some food for the world, promptly climbed down to the table, by way of the already shredded curtains, and joined us. Bread, eggs, or tomatoes were all fair game for him, and a little chattering conversation hit the spot too. Tulko, like all pet budgies, have pretty varied diets and can eat fruits, vegetables, seeds, as well as a number of human food items, like eggs and cheese. After eating and playing with Tulko, we went ahead and exchanged our gifts. Angelina presented me with a beautiful, black and brown sweater, and a matching scarf. "Well done. I like the color, and the size fits nicely too. Thanks!" I said politely and stole a quick kiss on her cheek.

She had great taste, not only in art but also in fashion. That much I had noticed the first time I laid my eyes on her. Likewise, she seemed happy with my gifts. "That's fantastic, I really like all of it. The jacket fits well too. Thank you so much. It will certainly come in handy", she said gratefully, after she opened the two packages, and tried the jacket on. I got a big kiss before she even took the jacket off. "This is how I'm going to hold you in this new jacket," she said excitedly, holding me tight from behind as if sitting on a bike. "Just the way I showed you in the park that night", she said teasingly. "Do you remember"? "How could I ever forget the best night of my life?" I replied jokingly.

Tulko had not been forgotten either, but only got a present from Angelina. It came in the *form of a large, three-kilogram bag of Neophema Parakeets food. Deeply embarrassed by my howler, I apologized to Angelina and promised to make it up to him, in the nearest future.*

For Christmas lunch, Angelina served Kutia, a traditional dish, made from cereal, raisins, honey, and other ingredients, garnished with poppy seeds, and carefully adorned in the shape of a star. She had prepared it the night before, while I was peeling potatoes. It turned out delicious, needless to say.

Contrary to our assumption, we didn't end up eating that Christmas lunch alone, after all. Tulko decided to join us at the table again. This time, he flew straight down, landed right on the rim of the bowl containing Kutia, and was about to help himself, if it wasn't for Angelina's quick reaction. She carefully frightened him off of the dish, lest he ended up in it. She then put a spoonful of it on a little coffee plate, and placed it on the table, near us. Like a true family member, he then ate his Christmas lunch along with us, in an orderly fashion.

In order to create that authentic Christmas atmosphere while eating, we took turns playing Christmas songs on our mobiles. A couple in Czech, several in Ukrainian, and a few in Russian, and English. Not to be outdone, Tulko sang along with some of the songs, resulting in both of us cracking up. The Christmas lunch ended up being special for the two of us. Unorthodox, but cheerful and happy.

It was time to call our families on WhatsApp.

We started off by calling Angelina's mom and brother. "Merry Christmas"! We said cheerfully, gave our best wishes, and showed our tree. "We've already bought presents for both of you, together with Tomas, and we will give them to you when you come to Mariupol in May", Angelina told them excitedly. Knowing I had no part in that, I knew Angelina told them a white lie. It made no difference anyway and was just a nice thing to say. "Likewise, we have one for

Tomas too, please tell him", her mother said proudly.

We repeated a similar type of conversation with my parents, exchanging best wishes and niceties. "I didn't know Angie, as my mom called Angelina, could cook Czech food too", she joked. "I did my homework", Angelina replied politely.

Last but not least, we talked to Angelina's grandparents too, but only on a regular phone, since they did not have a 4G or wi-fi connection at home. Wishing them nice Christmas, and introducing myself, at the same time.

Once finished talking with our families, it was time to call our closest friends. No one came closer than Herbert, since Olga was coming over in person anyways.

"We want to wish you the best Christmas ever", we joked, squeezing both our faces in front of the selfie camera. "Merry to the two of you too, and someone special wants to make a wish as well", said Herbert with an impish smile, as he was adjusting his selfie camera, to include a

*good-looking woman in its range. "This is
Oksana, my friend", he said casually. Oksana
was a good-looking woman in her mid-twenties,
with thick black hair dyed bright red, a fancy
low cut, red dress, penetrating eyes, and a thick
gold necklace. She wished us Merry Christmas
and hurriedly passed the phone back to the
beaming Herbert. Knowing him, and his unusual
dating ways, we knew better than to ask too
many questions. Certainly not in front of him, or
anyone else who knew him well. We were
certain she was his current lover. The reason we
had not met her before was that Herbert just
could not stick with the same lover for too long.
For this reason alone, he was not married in the
first place. At least he was honest with himself,
as well as with his partners. "Better than
making promises one does not keep", Angelina
and I readily agreed. That's why we both liked
and respected him in equal measure. Not to
mention the fact it was him, who hooked the
two of us up, in the first place.*

*Angelina did her homework on multiculturalism,
went out of her way to find out what the Czechs*

like to eat at this time of year, and she prepared fried fish with potato salad for Christmas dinner.

Before dinner, we took selfies in front of the Christmas tree to send to families and friends. Some were with Tulko on my head, some with Angelina kissing him, some with him sitting on top of the tree, and some with all three of us. Time flies when you're having fun, and before we knew it, the doorbell rang.

"What a nice, big tree you guys have", Olga observed excitedly, upon entering the living room. Andrey agreed and added. "This is from both of us, hope you guys make good use of it", and handed Angelina a gift, wrapped in a fancy, red and blue foil.

They had bought us a little coffee maker, which I was particularly fond of. "Much appreciated, and very handy," I said happily, checking the little machine out. In turn, Angelina presented Olga with a silver bracelet, and Andrey with a 128 GB micro SD card, both wrapped up in a single, purple-colored box.

"Let's move over to the kitchen now, where a traditional Czech Christmas dinner will be served now", said Angelina sweetly, with an impish smile on her face, and a discreet wink reserved just for me. Come to think of it, there wasn't anything particularly difficult, or unusual about this dish. Czech Christmas dinner usually consisted of a fried carp, or any other available fish, and potato salad anyone could really make. Still, I was happy it was being served, and by none other, than my beloved Angelina. Sure enough, it was well prepared. Whatever this girl did, she did it well, and I respected her for that. "Great job Angelina, even my mom doesn't make it this good," I joked, eliciting laughs from all of us. "Indeed, very tasty", our guests agreed, as they were munching on it. "Just watch out for bones", Angelina said cautiously. "Actually, Tomas was helping me with it", she acknowledged hesitantly. Well, since I only peeled the potatoes, I just nodded my head and smiled. After finishing dinner, Andrey pulled out a bottle of Uzvar, home-made by his father, and poured us all a glassful. "Here is to Christmas

everyone"! He said in a festive manner and took a swig from his glass.

The girls and I followed and then had some more. Stimulated by its good taste, and its alcohol content, we could not resist telling them about Oksana. As we were describing here, they both started giggling, and we joined them. There wasn't anything strange, or negative about her. Not at all. But Herbert's private life, especially his love life, had fascinated everyone who knew him. No one had any doubts he was a great man, a good friend, a great engineer, or an excellent CEO. There was just that something inherently funny about his ways, his mannerism, and we were all kind of hooked on it. We had even overheard naughty nicknames, like 'Herbert-The-Pervert', etc. But even those were meant in a positive light. No one actually tried, or wanted to insult him. On the contrary, we all liked him and didn't want him to change for the world. Simply put, he was a character larger than life.

Olga's and Andrey's visit, along with the WhatsApp calls had enlivened our first Christmas Day together and made it feel complete.

In the evening, after all the festivities had ended, Angelina and I turned off all the lights in the apartment, leaving only the Christmas tree lights to flicker. It was magical. We settled down on the sofa, covered ourselves with a blanket, turned on some soft music, cuddled up to each other, and just sat there like that for a while. Tulko, being an old budgie, had fallen asleep in the kitchen, in his open cage. Our first Christmas together turned out beautifully, and I felt I made the right decision to settle down in Mariupol, with Angelina by my side.

Time flies when you're having fun, and before we knew it, the Christmas holiday was over.

A person who never made a mistake never tried anything new.

XIII. The New Year

A couple of days before the New Year, Angelina suggested that we take a quick trip to Berdyansk, visit her old classmate who had invited us, pick up some art materials she no longer needed, and Angelina could use for school.

She also suggested, to my surprise, that we go there by motorcycle, pending the road and weather conditions. Otherwise, we'd take public transport. Angelina was not only eager to fetch the art materials, but also to finally take a proper ride, and introduce me to her friend.

After some discussion about the additional gear we'd need for the trip, we agreed to try it.

Because both myself, and Angelina were keen to ride the bike, even in wintertime, we checked out the weather forecast for the end of December 2021, and the beginning of January 2022. It turned out better than expected, to our big relief. The temperatures were predicted to hover around three to four degrees Celsius, with no rain or snow. "Bingo," I exclaimed enthusiastically. We got seated around the kitchen table, our favorite hangout at home, and created a plan of action. We knew it would be about an hour's ride, and despite already having good winter gear, we'd need to get a couple more items. The first is a set of new, winter tires, and the second is full windproof face masks. While the masks were not as essential as the tires, without them the trip would be a pain. "In summer, they absorb sweat and protect from the sun, while in winter they protect from wind and cold," I explained carefully. "Let's do it, what are we waiting for?" Angelina asked cheerfully, clutching my hand. That's why I loved this girl so much. On the one hand, she was responsible and caring. On the other, she was wild and adventurous. "What an amazing combination!" I thought. I placed my wallet in my front pocket, put on our riding gear, and set out to the bike shop. To keep the bike warm in wintertime, and protect it from the ever-curious kids, Angelina had struck a deal with a neighbor, allowing us to park the bike inside his garage, next to his car. Considering the garage was just around the corner from our building, it was a sweet deal, for a thousand Hryvna a month.

We were walking to the garage slowly and clumsily, dressed in full winter riding gear, complete with bulky shoes, gloves, helmets, and backpacks. I couldn't help the funny feeling we kind of looked like Buzz Aldrin and Neil Armstrong walking on the moon. The kids had a kick out of it too, and by the time we pulled the bike out and started it up, a dozen kids had assembled around the garage to enjoy the show.

There were plenty of face masks to choose from at the shop, and it took us less than five minutes to get some.

More importantly, we also bought new winter tires. To put them on, we rode to the same bike repair shop where they did the initial service for me. Once there, Angelina removed her helmet and let loose her long, blond, hair.

I immediately noticed how lustfully the mechanics were staring at her, trying hard as they might not show it. I couldn't blame them. With her hair swaying, dressed in her fancy riding gear, she looked as gorgeous as a reincarnation of a Hollywood actress, in the prime of her career.

We were sitting on empty crates, drinking some instant coffee they had offered us, while the guys were changing the tires. Half an hour later, we were cruising down Primorsky Boulevard, covered in new facemasks, on a bike with new tires. Now, we were ready for the trip to Berdyansk.

On the morning of December 27th, we set out at nine o'clock. The roads had not been frozen at night, and the frost always melted away quickly, under the tires of cars. As soon as the sun came out, the roads would dry up completely. Overcome by the excitement of our first proper ride, we were ready to hit the road.

The new tires stuck to the road like glue, so I felt confident to crank it up a notch. Soon, we were cruising at around 140 km/hour, overtaking almost everything on the road in front of us. After about 20 minutes of riding, I still did not feel any cold at all, so I assumed Angelina would not either, but I double-checked. "Are you feeling cold yet?" I called out to Angelina through my helmet, as I slowed the bike down for the purpose. "Not at all", she yelled back and squeezed me even tighter around the waist. Encouraged, I cranked it up again, and soon we were cruising at around 150 km/h. I only slowed down when reached the city limits. In less than 40 minutes, we reached Berdyansk safe and sound, before we could even get cold.

In the city center, we parked the bike, got off, and Angelina was beaming with happiness. I was relieved that our first long ride together went without a glitch. Not only did it go trouble-

free, but was exciting as well. "You were right about the face masks, you know. And about the tires too", she added observantly. "Thanks, I've been riding for years, and I know a thing or two about it," I replied self-assuredly. "I loved the ride, it was so exciting, and safe too. Thanks!" Angelina said excitedly. We parked the bike in front of the agreed restaurant in town, sent a message, and waited for Victoria, or Vika, as Angelina had referred to her. Vika showed up a bit late, all apologetic, carrying a big plastic bag, full of stuff. "I thought you guys would arrive later", she said apologetically. "Well, did you see that little rocket parked outside"? Angelina asked enthusiastically. "Besides, Tomas doesn't know how to ride slow anyways", she added jokingly. "You guys look so good in that gear", Vika replied somewhat enviously, but in good faith. "Makes me want to get a bike too", she joked. "This lunch is on me", Angelina said firmly, in a sign of gratefulness to Vika, for bringing all the art stuff she needed quite urgently at school.

"Anyone wants anything particular"? Angelina asked calmly, before ordering. "Up to you," we both indicated without hesitation.

Angelina had ordered Salo and Olivie, which was quite tasty, and all of us shared. The two ex-classmates-turned friends had a long, cordial chat after lunch. Vika then slowly got up, kissed Angelina on the cheeks, shook my hand, and said before leaving; "Very nice to meet you Tomas, and wish both of you the best of luck in the New Year. Do stop by again sometimes, whenever you guys like".

Angelina, eager to show me a thing or two in town before riding back, suggested taking a short ride around this place. The mini-tour was interesting. Berdyansk had a large naval base, an old lighthouse, and a similar coastal feel as Mariupol.

While our ride back felt as exciting and rejuvenating as our ride there, I noticed one of the cylinders missed a few beats. "No biggie, both spark plugs are old, and need replacement," I explained to Angelina assuredly.

Refreshed and satisfied, we cleaned ourselves up and hunkered down on the sofa. We stayed there for the rest of the evening. Relaxing, cuddling, and eventually making love. A fitting end to our first proper bike ride together.

The next morning, while still in bed, Nikolai let everyone know through our group WhatsApp, that he'd be hosting a special, New Year's Eve party at the Harbor Café. All-inclusive, with a 1200 Hryvna admission fee per head. "Fancy going?" I asked Angelina curiously, putting the tip of my index finger on her cute nose. "Absolutely", Angelina murmured sleepily, a brief smile appearing on her face. She then tucked herself in again, turned her back toward me, and went to sleep some more. I let her sleep and moved over to the kitchen.

My mobile started beeping incessantly, as various people started responding to Nicolai's invitation. Last but not least, Herbert requested a reservation for a party of two, launching the ex-pat gossip machine into overdrive.

*"Who is she, or he? Do you know Tomas?"
Various people fired off text messages, making
my phone busier still. No one knew for sure,
adding an element of surprise to the event.*

*On the 31st, the party officially started at seven,
but most people tended to show up later.
Angelina and I showed up at eight. She wore a
long pink dress, high heels, and a warm jacket
with a white, furry lining. I put on my usual dark
blue velvety jacket, light blue shirt, black pants,
and black shoes. Everyone would dress up a bit
better for the occasion, we assumed. Only Jack
was already present when we arrived, dressed
up in a black suit, white shirt, and a bowtie.
Shortly, others started arriving. Then came
Herbert, looking like a million bucks, his large,
light blue x-ray eyes checking out the scene,
with a beaming smile on his face.*

*He was walking arm in arm with a tall, shapely
woman, around twenty-five years old, adorned
with a thick gold necklace, and an expensive
Louis Vuitton bag slung over her shoulder. Her
hair was dyed brightly red, and braided into a*

long pony tail, looking like she had just stepped off a Milan catwalk. There was a brief, awed silence when they made their entrance, but that dissipated as soon as Herbert said aloud, cheerful hello to everyone around. "This is Oksana everyone", he introduced her lavishly. She briefly waved her hand, smiled, and they took their seats at our table. Despite Herbert's best efforts to present a normal, conventional lifestyle, it was anything but. Deep down, I knew all too well, that the date with Oksana was more of a mutual Pro-forma arrangement for the occasion, rather than a serious relationship. Despite that, or perhaps because of it, the party got a boost, became more mysterious, and more fun.

Nikolai had hired an extra waitress for the occasion, to make sure things went smoothly, resulting in speedier, friendlier service, and a better mood. He was also dressed up for the occasion, wearing a black suit, and a white shirt with a bowtie. It almost appeared like he and Jack shared the same tailor.

First, he made a small speech, wishing us all luck and happiness in the New Year, and he thanked us for our friendship and patronage.

After this, he asked the staff to bring out the hors d'oeuvres, and the party got officially going. One could see Nikolai made sure the food was good. The ingredients were fresh, expensive, and plentiful, resulting in the hors d'oeuvres tasting fantastic. Even Jeremy, the fussiest of eaters, had agreed. Australian Chardonnay was served to wash it down. Each additional glass seemed to make the mood merrier, and the voices louder, in almost direct proportion. Nikolai made sure there was a large enough space left open for dancing near the tables, which came in handy once a hired band started playing. Herbert took Oksana for dance first. Moving smoothly like Fred Astaire, he managed to break the ice, and soon enough, more people followed. I had never seen Jack dance before, but tonight he had managed to get a young Ukrainian lady to dance with him. After several glasses of wine, I didn't dance so badly either, at least according to Angelina and Herbert.

When the band took a break, with all of us seated around the table again, Jack suddenly dropped a bombshell, under the influence of alcohol.

"So, how did you two meet?" He mumbled haltingly, and with alcohol-glazed eyes, stared straight at Oksana and Herbert.

For a second, there was stone silence. This was a question no one was supposed to ask. It was an unwritten rule everyone had abided by, in our circle of friends. But when Jack was drunk, he was a straight shooter, being a soldier as he was. Fortunately, Herbert's mind was as sharp as a barber's razor, even when drunk. "She is a business associate at the port", he said calmly, but loudly enough for all to hear. Everyone present knew it was complete baloney, and none more so than Andrey, who worked at the office with Herbert. In order to negate Jack's obvious, drunken faux pas, and support Herbert, he said resolutely; "Yes, she is our business associate". An immediate relief could be seen on Oksana's face, but she remained silent. Herbert, who could not care less about himself, only tried to save Oksana from embarrassment. With this mini-crisis averted, and the clock nearing midnight, Nikolai had staff bring out several bottles of chilled Champagne and new glasses. He waited a couple of minutes, then asked the waitresses to pop the corks. Just before the clock struck midnight, they poured some into everyone's glass. Standing up and holding his glass raised, Herbert triumphantly exclaimed; "Happy New Year everyone", as the clock struck midnight. We all stood up and shouted Happy New Year. Angelina embraced me and gave me a nice sweet kiss. I reciprocated by embracing and holding her tight for a moment. We all then stepped outside on the terrace to watch the fireworks going off at the port. Their reflection could be seen on the calm surface of The Sea of Azov, enhancing the show. People were exchanging best wishes for the New Year, hugging each other, and shaking hands. What a magnificent, memorable evening

*it had turned out to be. I felt happy and grateful
I had Angelina, a bunch of good friends, as well
as an apartment in this town.*

*War is only a cowardly escape from the problems of
peace.*

Thomas Mann

XIV. The Getaway

*Having spent the Christmas and New Year
holidays busy doing things and going places, we
didn't mind taking it easy now, for a while.
Angelina and I took leisurely walks by the sea,
finally saw a show at The Drama Theater, and
visited the Kuindzhi Art Museum, among other
things.*

*Several weeks had passed since the beginning
of the New Year, and we finally had the time to
turn our attention to refurbishing our new*

apartment. Both the kitchen and bathroom were our top priorities, in dire need of repairs and upgrades. Changing the old, wooden windows for new, plastic ones, could wait till spring, as changing them in the dead of winter wasn't the smartest idea, we readily agreed. Duly, we ordered the services of a plumbing company to replace the toilet, all the faucets, and the shower, along with the pipes. The whole package was quoted to cost 18.000 Hryvna, which we paid for, and selected the new items through the company's online catalog. It was to be done, hopefully, in one day, but the company said it might take two, in case there were unexpected complications. Angelina and I agreed to invite them on Friday, and reserve the Saturday for possible extra work.

On Friday morning, four plumbers dressed in blue uniforms with the company's logo sewn neatly on them showed up as agreed, carrying several huge bags, full of equipment and tools. They took measurements, turned off the water supply, pulled out their hammers, and started *banging so loud, that I had to excuse myself. The company was to inform me via a text message in case they could not finish the job by 5 pm. In the meantime, I went to the bike repair shop to change the spark plugs, which they did. The engine did become more responsive, but it still missed a beat, here and there. "Eventually, the head gasket would need to be replaced, and if that didn't do the trick, the whole engine would need rebuilding," I figured. Considering the bike still ran fairly well, it was wintertime, and we had no plan to ride anywhere far at this point, I decided to do it all in spring.*

It was time to pick Angelina up, but I still had not received any message. Then, before she could even get on the bike, a message came, confirming they would need to work on Saturday as well. It was time for plan B.

Instead of going home, we rode straight to the Harbor Café and reserved 'Herbert's' room for the night. Tired, Angelina went straight upstairs to take a shower and get some rest, while I joined Jack and Nikolai downstairs. They were in the middle of a heated conversation. When they saw me approach, they turned down the heat a notch, but I asked anyway. "What's all this fuss about?" Cautiously, so as not to cause panic, they informed me that the negotiations between Russia and NATO weren't going well and that some airlines started canceling flights to Ukraine.

It was February 12th, and KLM had just announced their cancellation of flights to Ukraine. Unfazed, I responded confidently; "I heard the Russian government said they had no intention of invading Ukraine. Isn't that so?" "Yes, we heard that too, but", Nikolai replied haltingly.

At this point, he was getting visibly agitated. With a stern look on his face, he said; "Even though I am proud of my Russian heritage, I am a Ukrainian, I was born here, and this is my home. If they come here again to cause trouble, I will defend this town, and this country". He then walked to the café's back room, and a minute later came back with an old, but well-

kept, gleaming AK-47. He placed it firmly on the table in front of us with a determined expression on his face, as I had never seen him before. Jack picked it up with the touch of an expert, inspected it, stared down its barrel, and then put it back on the table. "Nice one", he said and nodded his head approvingly. It sent shivers down my spine. I knew there were tensions with Russia. It had been like that since 2014, after all. So, I never paid much attention to it, always assuming those issues had been settled, and all these troop movements were merely saber-rattling. But this time it was different. What I had witnessed here now, had spooked me. For the first time since moving to Ukraine, I became seriously concerned. On the one hand, I was happy to be with Angelina at the hotel for the night. But on the other, I kept worrying about how things might develop.

"What's the matter with you tonight?' Angelina asked worryingly and looked me straight in the eye. Clearly, I wasn't acting my usual self, and she had noticed. "Are you worried about the situation with Russia"? She asked again directly.

"Oh, it's nothing, I just feel tired tonight," I replied matter-of-factly, but untruthfully. On Saturday, at noon, we returned to the apartment. The work had been completed nicely, and all we needed to do was to clean up the mess and throw out the garbage they had left behind. The bathroom looked much better now.

Excited that our apartment was becoming modern and comfortable, we decided to give the shower a try. It worked beautifully, with stronger water pressure and hotter water too. Unfortunately, my excitement was short-lived. Soon, I found out that another airline, this time a Ukrainian Sky-Up, rerouted its flights from Kyiv to Moldova. Something was definitely up. While I didn't want to scare Angelina unnecessarily, I just had to have a word with her about the situation, whether I liked it or not.

As if all the flight cancellations had not been enough, a large number of countries had advised their citizens to leave Ukraine, and not to travel there for the foreseeable future. They included Czechia, Britain, the US, Norway, Germany, the Netherlands, etc. Some embassies had even told the families of diplomats to leave, as far back as January. Even one of the publications I worked for advised me to pack up and go. At this point, I sat down with Angelina, opened a bottle of Vodka to calm the nerves down, and had a serious talk. Neither one of us knew how all this might turn out, or more importantly, what we should do. An uneasy feeling suddenly descended upon us, ruining the otherwise happy life we've had here together.

Only Tulko was still being his old self, hopping around the kitchen table happily, shriek-talking as usual, livening up the gloomy atmosphere. The next day, Jeremy had called to say he was being transferred to Poland for a couple of months, ostensibly for training, and that they'd be leaving the next day, spooking us further still.

On Sunday morning, Andrey with Olga paid us an unannounced visit. Unusual as that was, they were always welcome in our apartment.

Angelina prepared coffee from the machine they had gifted us for Christmas, and almost inevitably, the conversation veered off the common pleasantries, and toward the rather dramatic situation with Russia.

Olga's feelings about the whole situation closely mirrored that of Nikolai, to Andrey's relief. If their relationship could survive this unfortunate episode, it could survive anything. Olga said she felt deeply embarrassed by the behavior of the Russian government, and that even her grandparents in Sochi didn't approve of it. She didn't want it to affect her friendship with Angelina, let alone her relationship with Andrey, and she let it be known. In turn, they both had reassured her it would not, no matter what might happen next. And so had I.

After a while, Andrey suggested that I go with him to the Harbor Café, to meet the boys for a chat, leaving the girls home alone for a while. While walking along the beach, Andrey was telling me how much he loved Olga, and that he was determined to fight, if it came to it.

All the guys showed up except Jeremy, as he had already been recalled by his employer, and was busy packing at home. Nikolai, Jack, Herbert, and a couple of American guys with cropped hair and muscular bodies that I had never met before, were there. I immediately understood this was no longer a joke, and that the perfect storm was brewing on the horizon.

They led us to Nikolai's backroom to show us an entire arsenal of weapons. Small arms, assault weapons, AK-47s, bazookas, hand grenades, etc. Jack told us the weapons were there in case Russia invaded, and if we decided to take up arms to defend the city. When I returned home that evening, the girls were still busy talking. Apparently, Andrey had told Olga to leave Ukraine for a while, or at least Mariupol, while he would stay and defend it, if necessary. None of us really believed a war would break out, despite warnings by the Americans.

The mere fact so many embassies were being evacuated, flights canceled, and companies recalling staff, gave us sleepless nights, however. Later in the evening my mother called and asked to speak to both of us. "Angie, why don't you and Tomas visit us for a while? We have a spare bedroom in our house, and you can stay as long as you want. It would be our pleasure to have you. Tomas, we want both of you to come home, as soon as possible. I am very worried", she told me, her voice trembling. "We are already considering it mom," I replied soothingly. Angelina also received a call from her mom later that night, saying she should come to Batumi with, or without me if necessary, and stay for a while until the situation calms down.

We didn't get any sleep that night. All we did was talk about what we should do, when, and how to do it. Eventually, we came up with a plan. If the situation had not improved by the end of the month, we would take a train to Poland, and fly to Prague from there. We'd stay at my folks' house until things got sorted out, and calmed down.

Armed with a plan, we could now breathe a little easier. Just to be on the safe side, I went to the train station on Monday the 21st, and bought three first-class tickets from Mariupol to Lviv, with a transfer in Kyiv, scheduled for the 28th. One was for Olga, in case she decided to join us. Olga thanked us and agreed to join if things got more heated. "Really nice of you guys. I'll be glad to join, but hope it won't come to that," she added nervously.

With one thing settled, another major scare popped up. And this one had a profoundly negative effect on both Angelina and I. Herbert just called to say his company was transferring him outside Ukraine, temporarily. Effective Wednesday the 23rd, he, along with a couple of colleagues from his office, would be heading to Hungary by car. "I could make two small folding seats in the back of the SUV available for you guys if you like", he said cautiously. "But you could only take a very limited amount of luggage with you. There won't be much room available in the car, but I think you should come. The situation in Ukraine doesn't look good. Let me know by Tuesday afternoon if you come", he added seriously. "We appreciate your offer very much, and we'll let you know by tomorrow afternoon", I replied nervously. Once again, Angelina and I started an earnest discussion.

"Very few things... What does he mean by that"? Angelina inquired curiously. "In a train, we could take most of our clothes, valuables as well as Tulko in his cage. I think we'd be better off taking the train. We'd be more comfortable, and besides, we already have the tickets anyways", Angelina concluded. "Even though the ride with Herbert would be safer and more fun, we could not take much with us. So you have a good point," I added uneasily. "Let's settle it then. We'll take the train if it becomes absolutely necessary. Besides, it still might not," I said resolutely. "Settled then", Angelina replied, also uneasily.

It was Tuesday, time to let Herbert know, one way or another. "We'll stick around a bit longer. Our train tickets have already been reserved, *and if this thing doesn't get sorted by the end of the month, we'll be on our way too. Thanks for everything, and keep in touch!" I told Herbert reluctantly.*

"Good luck my friend! I hope both of you stay safe, and we meet right here in Mariupol again", he replied as optimistically, as always.

Herbert, along with some of his colleagues had left early the next morning. Come Wednesday, I suddenly felt like my whole little world was coming undone. With many of my closest friends already gone, the Harbor Café now more resembling an ammunition depot than a café, and Angelina feeling blue, I struggled to keep my composure. Only Jack, Andrey, Olga, and Nikolai still remained, from our closest circle of friends. Even though I was trying to put a brave face on it, I fooled no one.

"Let's go to the mall. What do you say?" I asked Angelina warmly.

*"We can invite Olga and Andrey to tag along,"
I added suddenly, in the hope of cheering her up
a bit.*

*The sheer mention of Olga and Andrey did cheer
her up, and we decided to go. But only Olga
showed up. "Andrey and Jack went someplace
to train. I hope you don't mind", she said
casually. "Not at all", Angelina assured her
calmly. As we were walking through the mall, I
noticed people were withdrawing money from
ATMs, and long lines started forming. "Why
don't you two sit at that café, while I withdraw
some cash from an ATM," I suggested
unexpectedly. After about fifty minutes of
waiting in line, I finally managed to withdraw
thirty thousand Hryvna, and immediately
changed twenty thousand into Euro at an
atrocious rate, at a nearby money changer, just
in case. Then, with my pockets full of cash, I
invited both of them for lunch at the Barbaris to
liven up a bit and cast the gloomy thoughts
away. It did us good. We shared a large
pepperoni pizza, washed it down with beer,
then knocked back a few vodkas, and all of a*

sudden, our mood improved markedly. We exchanged a few jokes and expressed optimism that the situation won't be as serious as some suggested. Feeling relaxed and relieved, we returned home late that evening. In no time, we ended up making love. It was long overdue, and it brought back our lost enthusiasm for life. For the first time during that whole week, we fell asleep easily, cuddling and holding each other, just the way we used to.

When I woke up to go to the toilet that night, still hungover, I heard loud bangs and booms coming from a distance, complete with flashes of light. "Some storm, been a while since we had rain," I thought. I poked my head out the window but saw no rain. "Strange weather," I wondered cautiously. Having already been woken up by all the noise, I took my phone off the charger and turned it on, as I do first thing in the morning every day, after waking up.

As soon as the phone came on, I saw two messages from Jack.

The first message read; "Russia has attacked Ukraine, not far from Mariupol". The second went; "We won't be able to hold them off for too long. Get out and head west immediately, by any means possible. Good luck"!

Absolutely stunned, with cold sweat forming on my forehead, I went to wash my face, then read the messages again.

I had no choice but to wake Angelina up rather forcefully and tell her the news. Sleepy and terrified, she immediately sprung to action and started packing. "Take only the most important things," I told her. I put all my cash in my wallet, grabbed some clothes, and placed them in my suitcase, along with all of our new riding gear. Then I helped Angelina pack. We ended up with two large suitcases, two large backpacks, and Tulko in his cage. We closed all the curtains, turned off water, electricity, and gas, locked the doors, and down the elevator we went. I managed to flag down a taxi to take us to the station. It was almost six-thirty by the time we got there, and it was already packed with panicky people, loaded with all sorts of large luggage and various pets. The line for tickets was long, and we had no choice but to queue. It wasn't even our turn when the ticket office announced that all tickets for today had been sold out. They could only sell tickets for the train departing the next day. Stuck between a rock and a hard place, I was offering to buy people's tickets for this train at five times their price, then ten times, and even twenty times. There were no sellers, and belatedly, the urgency of the situation had dawned on us. "Let's try to hitch a ride in some car heading toward Berdyansk, or Dnipro", Angelina quickly suggested. "Let's do it," I readily agreed. We managed to get a taxi to take us to the main, western exit road. There we tried to hitch a ride, waving wads of cash at the drivers. But all the cars were full of families and friends, further loaded by heaps of luggage, nearly covering their windows. No one had room for us. One car had offered to take Angelina only, but she declined. The cars were moving at a fairly slow pace, due to the huge traffic jam which had formed on this road, leading out of town. After about forty minutes of trying, I looked at Angelina and asked; "Are you thinking what I am thinking?" "Let's take the bike", she said quickly and resolutely.

"Let's get rid of all the unnecessary luggage right here. Just take all the riding gear, the most essential stuff, and Tulko. There, in the garage, I saw a shoebox. We'll poke holes in it, and put him in our backpack," I said determinedly. "Let's do it"! Angelina said firmly, without hesitation. We threw away most of our staff and kept only the riding gear, some essential stuff, and Tulko in his cage. Then, we quickly walked to the garage, which wasn't that far away, due to the location of our apartment, near the exit road. There, I realized I had left the garage keys in the apartment. Not to waste precious time, I found a rock nearby and pounded the lock till it snapped. The neighbor's car was no longer there, giving us more room to maneuver. Our helmets were hanging on the bike's handlebars where we left them, and we quickly changed into full riding gear. The Puma branded shoebox

I saw earlier, was still there. We quickly poked holes in it, put a piece of rag inside to absorb the shocks along the way, and placed the reluctant, panicked Tulko in it, against his will. We then placed it inside Angelina's backpack, and left a small part of the zipper open, for Tulko to breathe through. We placed the few remaining things in the top and side boxes of the bike. To our great relief, the bike managed to start, and off we went. A minute later, Angelina poked me in the side and said. "Now that we have the bike, I must stop by my mom's apartment real quick, turn everything off, and take our most important valuables. I almost forgot in this helter-skelter". Once we got there, she ran frantically towards the entrance, and returned in less than 20 minutes, clutching a plastic bag full of important documents and memorabilia, which she then placed in one of the side boxes. All the while, I kept the engine running, just in case. The last thing Angelina did before getting on the bike, was to send a quick text to Olga, telling her we missed the train, and are leaving on the bike instead, right now. She urged Olga to get out of town immediately, the any-which way she could.

Finally, we were on the exit road, passing all the cars stuck in the traffic jam, with relative ease. The booming sounds of artillery shells were getting louder, and some started landing not far behind us. It was terrifying, and we were completely exposed to the elements. I realized I had to get us out of there as quickly as I could.

One by one, we were getting ahead of the cars. Riding on the very edge of the road, Angelina was holding me tight, just the way she said she would, that night on our first date. The farther away from Mariupol we were getting, the lesser was the traffic, the faster our speed, and the quieter the bombs. Because no one knew how far and fast the Russians would advance, we didn't even have time to contact Vika, when we stopped to get gasoline in Berdyansk. Some stations were closed, and the few that were still open were busy with cars. We got lucky, and as soon as we filled up, we continued on our way to Zaporizhzhia and Dnipro. The roads outside of Mariupol were not nearly as busy as the exit road from it. Mariupol was only 20 miles from the frontline, and obviously was one of the first targets of the invasion. We considered ourselves very lucky to have gotten out, in the nick of time. But we worried about Olga, Jack, Nikolai, Andrey, and even Vika. We worried all of Ukraine might become occupied within days.

Getting to Melitopol only took us thirty-five minutes, and we filled up again. At the gas station, we bought some cotton, and placed it in Tulko's box for comfort and warmth, along with a piece of apple. We also gave him some water to drink from a bottle top. He was so stressed out that he barely touched it, poor soul. Even in Melitopol, we heard some shelling in the distance, but much further away than it was in Mariupol. We didn't take any chances, and quickly proceeded on the road toward Dnipro, only stopping in Zaporizhzhia at the gas station to eat something, use the toilet, and fill up. About two-thirds of the way towards Dnipro, I noticed that one of the cylinders started missing a beat with increasing frequency, resulting in a slightly jerkier ride. A bad sign by all means, as every biker knows.

I noticed the engine started losing power, ever so slightly. It meant the pistons were gradually losing compression, possibly even oil, and I already knew that the bike would eventually stall. But I still hoped we would make it to Dnipro, where mechanics were hopefully still available. I eased off on the throttle a bit but still kept going at least eighty km/h. We had to make it to Dnipro, a relatively safe place in the hinterlands, further away from the frontlines. There, we could pause, repair the bike, and spend the night. Despite our excellent riding gear, it was getting colder on the bike, after riding for hours. We now only had less than fifty kilometers to reach Dnipro, but unfortunately, the bike started losing more power. At first, I didn't even want to tell Angelina we had a mechanical problem until we reached the town. Five minutes later, however, the bike started slowing down and overheating. I was afraid the engine might seize completely. "What's the matter? Is anything wrong"? Angelina inquired nervously. I knew this was the end of the road for the bike, but I hated telling her the truth.

"This is it. We won't get any further on it. The bike needs an extensive engine repair. It's done." I replied anxiously. "Oh really? That's terrible! What are we going to do now"? Angelina asked worriedly and started getting off the bike. "Can it be fixed somewhere"? She asked repeatedly. "It can, but not quickly, not in this situation," I explained. I know you love the bike, and so do I. "We have no choice but to leave it here, and hitch a ride to Dnipro, then continue on our way. Unfortunately, we can't deal with the bike under these circumstances. At least the bike got us out of Mariupol, and we have to make it to Poland tomorrow. Who knows if, or how quickly the Russians overrun this place. I am really sorry." I said anxiously and started detaching the boxes from the rack. Even though we were on the main highway, we were in the sticks, and the nearest village of Pervomaiske was at least 20 km away, according to my google maps. At least the internet was still working, kind of, breaking up half the time. I explained to Angelina that even if someone was willing to transport the bike to Dnipro, we had limited cash on us, weren't sure if ATMs would be working, and didn't know how long the repair would take, or how much it would cost. After all, our first priority was getting to safety, and everything else was of secondary importance. Angelina understood the situation, nodded her head, but gave me a sad look. I took the side boxes, and carried the backpack with Tulko in it, while Angelina took the top box. It was getting late in the afternoon, and we had to hitch a ride to Dnipro, by any means available, as soon as possible. We kept walking, trying to hitch a ride, any ride. After about thirty minutes, a sympathetic driver of an off-duty Coca-Cola delivery truck took us and put us in his cargo area. It was full of crates, filled with empty coke bottles, rattling and clanking all the way to the outskirts of Dnipro, where he off-loaded us. From there, we saw a small motel in the distance. Exhausted and shell-shocked, we dragged our bike luggage for half a mile to get there. At first, the receptionist said they had no available rooms. After Angelina told him about our dramatic escape from Mariupol he relented, but only offered us the most expensive room. We immediately accepted. It wasn't easy to find a room, as hordes of desperate people, escaping the border areas, were coming into town, just like us.

As depressing as it was to have to abandon our beloved bike, it was also a wonderful feeling to have escaped a calamity of enormous proportions and be able to take a rest in a warm room, with a hot shower and all. We had the bike to thank for that, after all. Without it, we might not have been able to escape Mariupol in the first place.

The first thing we did after entering the room, was released Tulko from his box. Immediately, he started flying around the room, frantically shrieking and crashing into windows and doors. We felt sorry for him but were happy we even managed to get him out of Mariupol with us. He only calmed down, after Angelina started *talking and singing to him, and came down to sit on her shoulder.*

After taking a long hot shower together, I quickly left the hotel to find a couple of travel bags with wheels. Carrying the top boxes like that was too heavy and impractical. I managed to come across a Vietnamese-owned shop, selling multiple types of merchandise, as well as luggage. I quickly fetched a couple of midsize bags with wheels, large enough to fit all our things in, including helmets. I also bought a couple of pairs of underwear for both of us, a couple of t-shirts, and a small towel for Tulko, because we didn't have time to do any washing. The shop happened to have some empty boxes lying around, so I picked one up for Tulko. It was larger than his current box, but would still fit into the backpack, and would be more comfortable for him. On the way back, I picked up some pierogi, a bottle of Coca-Cola, some water, and apples. We were in no mood to go out and search for dinner. Even Dnipro was in a limited state of panic, but nowhere near the level of Mariupol, which was under direct attack at this point. After dropping off all the staff at the hotel, I rushed to the train station. I quickly managed to get a taxi, and after queuing for an hour, got us the tickets for the morning train to Lviv, via Kyiv.

Throughout the evening, with the hotel's Wi-Fi functioning, we kept receiving calls and messages from friends and family. Our mobiles were full of unanswered calls and messages from earlier in the day, and we were now finally in a position to give everyone concrete answers, regarding our situation.

We also received messages from Herbert and Jeremy. We tried to contact all of them. Despite our positive assurances, Angelina's mom was crying, but satisfied upon hearing from us. "Tomas, please, take care of Angelina, and get her home safe with you", she asked, choking in tears. "I will, I promise you that," I assured her boldly. My folks, too, were extremely relieved by our call. "Just get over here, both of you. Don't wait around anywhere, come straight here, no matter how much it may cost". My mom added eagerly.

Herbert, who had crossed into Hungary only this morning, was almost as concerned. "Wow, well done Tomas, glad you were able to get out of there, in the nick of time! I wish you had come with us", he added matter-of-factly. "Never mind the bike, you'll get a new one. Hope you can make it out tomorrow. If you need a place to stay for a while, you can stop by Vienna, any time". He informed us enthusiastically. We also sent a message to Jeremy and Sabrina, who were equally relieved to hear from us. One thing, however, bothered us all. Andrey, Olga, Nikolai, and Jack were not answering any messages or calls. We figured they were tied up in the defense of Mariupol, and we kept our fingers crossed for their safety.

From friends as well as online news channels, we found out that Kyiv, along with western Ukraine, was not yet under attack. Since we had already experienced an attack on Mariupol, we knew it was only a matter of time.

Angelina didn't waste any time, and while I was out at the station, had already packed our new bags, prepared new clothes for us to change into, and fixed up Tulko's new box for tomorrow's difficult journey.

By the time we settled into the bed, Tulko had calmed down, climbed down the curtains, and joined us. We fed him bread crumbs and pieces of apple, after which he drank water from the plastic bottle cap.

We placed his new, open travel box next to our bed, and surprisingly, he fell asleep in the new towel we put inside it.

The next morning, well prepared in advance, we got going early. It wasn't even five-thirty when we arrived at the station. Large crowds were gathering there already, mostly women with kids, and older people. But it wasn't as busy, or as frantic as it was in Mariupol the day before. Dnipro was not under attack and was relatively far from the front, that's why not everyone was leaving. But even there, people weren't sure what was to come next. As soon as they opened the train carriages, we proceeded to take our designated seats, to make sure we'd even get in. Shortly before the scheduled departure time, more people we pushing in, some without tickets. When we saw a woman without a ticket, with two small kids, carrying heavy bags, we squeezed ourselves onto the seat of our compartment, and let her join us. She put the girl on Angelina's legs, and the small boy on her lap. Pretty soon the train got moving, and we all breathed a sigh of relief. Then, just as we started falling asleep, Tulko decided to wake up. We began hearing grinding noises coming from his little beak, a sure sign of a parakeet's relative comfort. Having already gotten used to his new, larger box, he started making a medley of chirrups, and whistles and even started saying his trademark words of Zdrastvuj and Chorosho.

This got the attention of everyone in the cabin, especially the kids. They started laughing and repeating the words back to Tulko, who kept *repeating them. Suddenly, despite the subdued mood, and the difficult situation we were all in, a ray of light descended upon our cabin. The kids were laughing, looking at Tulko through the air vents in the box, and talking to him. Smiles began to appear on everyone's faces.*

Tulko had broken the ice and got everyone's mind off of the terrible events unfolding on Ukraine's borders.

Several hours later, we arrived in Kyiv. Tired, worried, but still in pretty good shape, we joined the crowds of people in the underground station and waited for the train to Lviv. Managing to escape from the jaws of death was the most important thing, regardless of the cost, we both agreed.

Despite Kyiv being surrounded by Russian troops on two sides, it still wasn't under a direct attack. Heavily defended, it was functioning in a semi-normal mode. While the crowds at the station were growing, and most people were stressed out, they were also orderly.

Having bought the tickets a day earlier, we were able to get on the train first. But hordes of other people without tickets were trying to get on as well. It was the twenty-fifth of February, a day after the invasion started, and no one knew if, or for how long Kyiv could hold out. The trains were still departing as scheduled, and ours left the station just after three pm. As earlier, we squeezed on our bench to let an elderly couple sit next to us. They carried a small black and white dog with them and clutched a couple of plastic bags. "They are on their way to Uzhgorod, a town close to the Slovakian border, where their son lives. Their house in Kharkiv had been damaged by a shell", Angelina told me quietly, wiping her tears. It was very hard for me to keep my composure, seeing the tragedy unfold, all around me. We were very relieved to have arrived in Lviv, never mind it was at half-past eleven at night. It didn't even matter if we couldn't find a hotel to sleep in. Just being in Lviv, far away from the frontline was a major victory for us. We were safe, along with Tulko, and we'd be able to start anew, be it in Czechia, or back in Ukraine, situation permitting. After arrival, we were wandering the streets of Lviv at night, along with scores of other, desperate refugees, looking for a place to rest through the night. Luckily, our new luggage was easy to haul on its wheels, and we were able to reach the city center quickly. Angelina spotted a small sign, advertising a room in a private house for rent, along with the address and phone number. Once again, we got lucky. One room was still available, and we booked it immediately. It was relatively a short walking distance away. We reached it dead tired but extremely relieved, checked in, took a hot shower, and ordered a hot meal from the family, which they had offered free of charge, in their kitchen. Tulko, who was patiently waiting for us in the room, got the leftovers. Without the owners' knowledge, we closed the window, locked the door, and let Tulko out. The poor thing started flying around anxiously, but less frantically than last night. He got somewhat used to this new, crazy way of life. In no time, he descended on the table, and started eating bread crumbs, and pasta and then nibbled at the grapes we brought in.

Knowing we had almost made it, we fell asleep quickly and easily. I had not woken up the whole night and only went to the bathroom in the wee hours of the morning. So tired were we, that we didn't leave the room till a quarter to twelve the next day. The family was friendly and understanding of our situation. They served us breakfast and even dropped us off at the bus station, from which we caught the 2 pm bus to the Shehyni / Medyka border crossing. The entire access road was overflowing with Ukrainian refugees, as well as foreigners caught up in the invasion, like me. We stood in line for hours and hours, with the border guards overwhelmed by the sheer numbers. There were kids crying, elderly people sitting on their luggage, fathers saying goodbye to their families, and people clutching their meager possessions and various pets. As frantic and sad as it was, it came as a relief to most, just to get out of the war zone. Exhausted, sweaty, and anxious, we finally made it across the Polish border. It was well past seven, and already getting dark outside, when we saw volunteers working for various aid agencies serving hot soup, and basic food for refugees. We helped ourselves to some soup, just to warm up. Being on the EU's and NATO's territory, we finally felt safe and breathed a huge sigh of relief.

"We did it"! Angelina exclaimed excitedly. Misty eyed, she put her head on my chest, and held on tight. "You bet we did!" I replied solemnly and embraced her tight. We stood there for a while, hugging each other. It didn't matter to us much anymore, whether we'd spend the first night in a hallway or a garage. We were now in safe territory, and from now on, we could start rebuilding our lives.

"Take a deep breath, pick yourself up, dust yourself off and start all over again."

Frank Sinatra

XV. The Aftermath

Shortly after crossing into Poland, we managed to get on a packed bus to Przemysl, the closest town to the border. After twenty minutes of being pushed and squeezed around, we were there. While we didn't have much money left, we did have some, unlike some other, less unfortunate refugees. I was able to withdraw several hundred Zlotys from a nearby ATM machine, enough to pay for hotels, trains, and buses, all the way to Prague. To help the refugees, several hotels in town were offering huge discounts, some were even free of charge. It was difficult, however, to find one with a vacancy. A large number of people were sleeping in lobbies, on sofas, or even on the floors. Fortunately, we managed to find a guesthouse with a vacant room, even though it was far from the center of town. It was a distance we were more than willing to go, in order to get much-needed rest. Even though we'd sleep in a lobby if we had to, we wouldn't pass up an opportunity to get proper rest, if it presented itself, as it did. Besides, it only cost 125 Zloty a night, a real bargain, under the circumstances. We needed to recover from this traumatic journey, both physically and mentally, and pull ourselves back together. Tulko also needed to be let out of the box for a while, something we could not do in a lobby. Despite feeling blue to have left our home behind, and losing our beloved motorcycle along the way, we felt extremely relieved to be safe.

No one had any idea at this point if, or when, Mariupol, Kyiv, and other cities might fall to the invaders. No one knew, if this was going to be an all-out war, or whether Ukraine would be able to resist the Russian juggernaut to some extent, at least.

No sooner than the hotel door was locked, and the windows were closed, we released Tulko from the confines of his makeshift birdcage. He flew around the room for a minute or two, then landed on top of the curtains, and settled in there. In the meantime, we took our long-awaited hot showers, and it never felt better. All our clothes were thoroughly filthy now, and since there was no time for having them washed, we decided to buy new ones, just for the road. We also needed a number of personal hygiene items, especially for Angelina. A new, larger travel cage for Tulko was an absolute must.

The guest house had a small restaurant, in which we had dinner, and brought bits and pieces for Tulko, as was the case all along this unplanned trip. The whole experience had been so tiring and traumatic, that we didn't even feel like making love that night, and just caressed and cuddled, instead. Tulko's presence was very important, especially for Angelina's state of mind. True, I might lose my new apartment if the war turns out badly for Ukraine, but

Angelina might lose her family's apartment, her hometown, and possibly even her country if all of Ukraine fell to the invaders. As the magnitude of this disaster began to dawn on me, I started comforting her, and looking after her, as best as I could.

Early in the morning, while Angelina was still sleeping, I went out shopping. The town was full of refugees, everywhere! I saw a mother with two small kids, one of whom was crying loudly, telling me she lost her house north of Kyiv due to shelling, and that she didn't have enough money to get to her friend's house in Warsaw. I opened my wallet, pulled out 200 Zloty, and said calmly; "This will get you all to Warsaw, and more." Overcome with joy, she started sobbing. Seeing that, I was fighting back tears myself. It was too much for me to deal with, but at least I helped out. Once the woman regained her composure, I wished her luck and proceeded to buy the things we needed most. Przemysl was a small town, and only had a limited selection of pet products. Under those circumstances, I got a smallish plastic box with holes, to serve as a temporary portable cage. I bought just enough clothes and personal items, to last us till we got to our new home, near Prague. Before returning to the guesthouse, I picked up train tickets to Wroclaw. From there, it wasn't that far to Prague. We rode a comfortable, long-distance bus, reaching our destination late that night. As agreed, my parents were waiting for us at the station. As soon as we disembarked, they hugged and kissed us, trying their best to make Angelina feel welcome. An hour later, we arrived at our family house in Kralupy nad Vltavou.

"Wow, you really have a nice house", Angelina said politely, upon arrival. "Is this for Tulko?" She asked curiously when my dad showed her a large enclosure in the hallway. "You bet it is", he answered obligingly. We promptly released Tulko into it. I had instructed my folks, before we arrived, to take extra care of Tulko, explaining how important he was to both of us, and especially to Angelina. To impress her, my dad had constructed a large, 1.5m x 2m enclosure for Tulko, complete with twigs to

perch on, and a birdhouse. He placed it in the hallway during winter, and it could be moved to the garden in summer.

While unpacking our bags in my room, which my folks had hastily rearranged to accommodate two, I noticed that Angelina had brought with her my beloved, faded pink t-shirt, as well as the blue jeans I saw her in, the night we met at Barbaris. She remembered I once told her to never throw them away. And she hadn't, even under the most critical circumstances. When I saw that, I came right over to her, kissed her, and squeezed her tight. She was a loyal partner, a trustworthy person, and a great artist, all in one. Not to mention the fact she was very attractive and great fun to be around. We quickly settled into our new home. Angelina and I were in my old room, while Tulko was in his new, large enclosure.

A friend notified us there was going to be an anti-war demonstration in Prague on the 26th, the next day, so we informed my folks we would be going early in the morning.

After dinner, which my mom painstakingly prepared for us, Angelina talked to her mom on WhatsApp for a while, saying all was fine now, sobbing briefly. She explained that we had taken the valuables from their apartment, before escaping. Angelina's mom expressed her thankfulness to my folks, for looking after us in these most difficult times. We then put the phone in front of Tulko, to say hello. He immediately recognized her mom's voice, perked himself up, and started shriek-chattering. Angelina's mom was so glad to see him that she started sobbing. Eventually, an agreement had been reached, that Angelina's mom and brother would visit here in June.

Angelina was visibly calmed down by the phone call, and by the fact, that she saw my parents went out of their way to make her feel welcome. Our first night here felt eerily similar to our first night in Angelina's apartment. Finally, we felt relaxed enough to make love, the way we used to.

Early next morning we took a train to Prague, to take part in the demonstration. The crowds were huge, many speeches were made. Most importantly, for Angelina, we had met many Ukrainians, some of whom exchanged their numbers with us. Angelina quickly made new friends with the people who understood her, and with whom she could share both happiness, as well as pain. One positive aspect of being in Czechia, for all Ukrainians, was the fact Czechoslovakia had also been invaded by Russia before, and the people here understood their plight.

After the demonstration, Angelina explained she had brought the rolled-up sketch of Mariupol, which she had intended to give to my parents as a gift, on our planned visit in June. Under these circumstances, however, she had no time to get it framed. We ended up going to Ikea, selected a suitable frame, placed the sketch in it, and had it gift wrapped.

"It looks amazing! Thank you so much. Did you do this by yourself, Angelina"? Asked my dad

curiously, while opening it up. He then took down a picture of the Czech countryside from our living room and replaced it with Angelina's Mariupol.

A couple of days later, we got an unexpected, but most welcome message from Andrey. He had informed us that Olga, along with some friends, had managed to get out of Mariupol by car, under heavy bombardment, and made it all the way to her friend's house, somewhere in a village west of Dnipro. Apparently, Nikolai, Jack, and Andrey were all battered and bruised, but alive and kicking, and all three would be withdrawing from Mariupol, and joining Ukrainian defensive positions further west. "Mariupol could no longer be defended under a constant, heavy, and concentrated attack by the enemy," he added solemnly.

"You did the right thing to have left on the bike immediately." He told us resolutely. "The train you tried to take on the 24th, was the last train from Mariupol. Later that night, the tracks were bombed, and the train service had stopped

indefinitely", he added haltingly. "I am afraid to inform you Angelina, and it breaks my heart, that large parts of Mariupol had been either badly damaged, or completely destroyed, beyond repair".

We could hear loud bangs in the background as he was speaking. "We can't get in touch with anyone in Mariupol, the connection doesn't seem to be working", Angelina said anxiously. "There is no longer electricity in parts of the country, so the signal doesn't get forwarded", he explained. Then, suddenly, the line got cut. We tried calling him back, in vain.

The only things we managed to save from Mariupol were some clothes, a handful of memorabilia, some documents, the sketch now hanging in the living room, and Tulko.

We still had wonderful memories though, good friends, as well as each other. We swore we'd return one day, whenever it became possible.

Index:

Cossacks : *https://en.wikipedia.org/wiki/Cossacks*

Hryvna : *https://en.wikipedia.org/wiki/Ukrainian_hryvnia*

Olyvie :

https://natashaskitchen.com/olivye-ukrainian-potato-salad/

Azovstal :

https://en.wikipedia.org/wiki/Azovstal_iron_and_steel_works

Printed in Great Britain
by Amazon

83329675R10153